Discovery in Great Sand Dunes National Park

National Park Mystery Series
Book Two

Aaron Johnson

ILLUSTRATED BY
The Author

COVER ILLUSTRATION BY
Anne Zimanski

HTTPS://NATIONALPARKMYSTERYSERIES.COM

Cover Artwork by Anne Zimanski

Illustrations by Aaron Johnson.

This is a work of fiction. Names, characters, organizations, historical events, and incidents are the products of the author's imagination. The roles played by historical figures and organizations in this narrative and their dialogue (while based on the known facts of their real lives) are also imagined. The only exception is Harold Westinghouse III, the squirrel at the end of chapter twenty-four. Harold has signed legal documents to testify that he was accurately portrayed in this narrative and does not hold the author liable for any misrepresentation of his character or actions.

Paperback ISBN: 978-0-9897116-7-8

Ebook ISBN: 978-0-9897116-8-5

To Mrs. Jones.
For igniting in me a love for reading.

Great Sand Dunes
National Park

Sangre De Cristo Mountains

Marble
Mountain

Liberty Gate

Mt. Herard • Medano
Lake

Medano
Pass

Sand Ramp Trail

Medano Pass Road

Dunefield

Sand Sheet

High Dune

Point of
No Return

Medano Creek

Piñon Flats
Campground

N

W   E

S

Park Entrance

To Zapata Falls
Recreation Area

Sangre De Cristo Mountains

One Mile

THE QUEST

Dear Reader,

Thirteen-year-old Jake Evans possesses something valuable: a scrapbook passed down to him by his grandfather, who used it to document his visits to sixty-two United States National Parks.

Inside the scrapbook, his grandfather hid clues, codes, maps, and riddles leading, first Jake, and now his cousin, Wes, and friend Amber, on a scavenger hunt through ten national parks.

But the three friends have learned that it's more than a game. For decades, his grandfather had been discovering hidden relics and signs in the national parks. Before his death, he had pieced enough of the clues together to realize he was uncovering an ancient mystery. Knowing he would die before solving the mystery, he entrusted his quest to Jake.

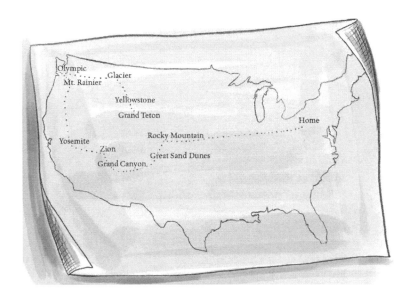

Last week, Jake's family traveled from Ohio to Colorado to begin a two-month vacation in the national parks—a trip his grandfather planned before his death. In Colorado, at Rocky Mountain National Park, Jake and his friends discovered two important clues. The first came in a package. Inside he found a heavy, old wooden box, locked with no apparent way to open it. In the package, he also found this note:

Burn the package and burn this note. THEY know I have it, and it's no longer safe with me. I'm number 23, which makes you Keeper 24. Here are the instructions I received from 22: You are its steward and protector, charged to keep it hidden. Discover what can be discovered and find the next Keeper. All we've learned has been entrusted to the Marmot.

The box remains locked. There's no keyhole or any other apparent way to open it. A letter from his deceased grandfather instructed Jake to "Keep it locked. You'll find the key in due time."

The second clue they found was a journal, over a century old, containing drawings of an ancient silver spearhead.

Silver Spearhead. Found at Dunraven Ranch, May 1880

Though Jake and his friends have no idea exactly what they are after, they know it must be valuable because someone else is after it, too. For decades, maybe even more than one hundred years, a shadow group has been on this same quest. They want the box and the journal. They need the scrap-book, and they'll do whatever is necessary to find and take them.

Enjoy the adventure,
Aaron Johnson, Author

CHAPTER 1

SUMMER 1880 - SANGRE DE CRISTO MOUNTAINS, COLORADO

"Find that mutt and put it out of its misery." The man sat upon a black horse and wore a black overcoat with silver buttons. Though he was high in the mountains, his shirt and tie were crisp and unworn compared to the clothes of his two companions. A pair of hounds circled the three horses, baying and eager to pursue their prey.

"Yes, sir. The hounds have its scent now, so I expect we'll find it by sundown."

The third man patted the revolver strapped to his side. "And then we'll dispatch the critter."

"I expect to see you two back at the mine tomorrow," the well-dressed man said, his voice firm. He jerked the reigns to turn his horse and disappeared into the forest.

"Emma!"

A girl of about sixteen appeared from behind the barn carrying two wooden buckets. Water sloshed over the rims of both, splashing a mix of dirt and water onto her dusty leather boots. The sweat on her forehead held fast several strands of strawberry blonde hair. A single braid swayed like a pendulum across the back of her button-up cotton shirt, which showed the unladylike signs of hard work. She set the buckets down on the steps of the house and shook the dust off the hem of her calico skirt.

"Yes, ma'am."

"I wondered where you had gone off to, that's all." The short older woman folded her muscular arms across her chest. Like most ranchers, she looked older than her true age, having been weathered by the sun and toil. Her blue collared shirt was spotless thanks to the long apron she wore over her clothes.

"Mrs. Herard, could I take my horse out this afternoon when I'm finished with the chores?"

"Yes, you may, child. But don't go off too far. I'll need your help with dinner."

"Thank you, ma'am. I'll be back in time."

Emma dragged several heavy rugs out of the ranch house and threw them over the clothesline to hit them with a wooden pitchfork. After sweeping and scrubbing the floors, she put the rugs back and then went to the barn to find her horse.

"Gideon, how are you, boy?" She ran her hand along the horse's side and then scratched his favorite spot, right between his eyes. Gideon was the last of her family. Emma's parents and siblings had perished two years ago in the blizzard of 1878. She laid her cheek against his. "It's just you and me this afternoon, boy. We can do what we please until dinner." Emma strapped a saddle on Gideon's back, slipped the bridle over his head, and led him out of the barn.

The vanilla scent of ponderosa pines filled the air, and the afternoon sun warmed Emma's skin. She looked through the trees to the north, where the golden hills of the sand dunes spread out below them. Gideon made a nickering sound. "Not today, boy. We'll visit the dunes again soon enough. Today, we're going into the mountains." She put her foot in the stirrup and climbed into the saddle.

They made their way along the Medano Pass Road, which followed the creek up into the mountains toward

Medano Pass. In the summer months, miners and settlers from the East used the road to cross the Sangre De Cristo Mountains.

Below the pass, Emma steered Gideon off the road and onto a trail that led up and into the forest. Because the way was dense with fir and spruce trees, she had to duck under branches and then guide Gideon over deadfall and around the giant boulders that choked their path. An hour later, they arrived at their destination, Medano Lake. Surrounded by mountains and snowfields, this alpine lake had become Emma's favorite place in the world. Here, the only sounds came from the birds and the wind.

Medano Lake

She tethered Gideon to a tree beside the water where he could drink, then walked across stepping stones to a boulder out in the lake. She sat down on the rock, wrapped her arms around her legs, and reveled in the beauty of the place. A breeze came down the mountainside and, like a spirit or the breath of God, jetted across the surface of the placid water.

A whimper interrupted the quiet. Gideon raised his head from the water and turned toward the sound. It came again, more of a cry this time. Emma stood, turned to the woods behind her, and listened. Gideon watched with concern. She walked back across the stones to the shore of the lake, then followed the sounds into the forest. In a thicket of brush and briars, she found the source of the cries.

A golden retriever lay on its side. A gash across one of its front legs turned his yellow fur red with blood. "Oh, you poor boy," she said. "What happened to you?" The dog's muzzle and head were scratched by briars, and its neck fur was matted with cockleburs.

She reached out her hand and touched his side. The dog whined, but he didn't snap. She studied his paws, all of them cracked and bleeding. "We need to get you some help."

His ears perked, and he turned his head to the north.

Emma turned to listen with him. From the ridge above the lake came the baying of hounds and the voices of men.

CHAPTER 2

PRESENT DAY - HAMBURGERS AND RIDDLES

"Hey, buddy, are you awake?" Jake's dad called back from the driver's seat.

Jake stretched and yawned, pulled the blanket off his chest, and sat up. Looking at himself in the rearview mirror, he could see that the hair on one side of his head was smashed flat, and the other side was springy and full of static. He tried to fix it, then gave up and put on his ball cap. "Where are we?"

"A few miles outside Buena Vista," his mom replied from the front passenger seat. "Uncle Brian says there's a good burger place here. We're going to stop for lunch in a few minutes."

The landscape had changed since that morning when they left Rocky Mountain National Park. Three hours had passed, and they were now deep in the middle of

Colorado, on a highway winding along the Arkansas River. A snow-laden mountain with three peaks dominated the landscape.

"What mountain is that?" Jake asked

"We've passed signs for Mount Harvard and one for Yale," his mom replied, "but I haven't seen a sign for *that* one yet."

A mile later, a rectangular green sign appeared on the side of the road. He leaned forward to read it: *Mt. Princeton, 14,196'.*

"Mt. Princeton." Jake sat back in his seat. "I wonder why they named these mountains after colleges."

Mt. Princeton

"I bet Wes knows." His dad winked at Jake in the rearview mirror.

Jake laughed. His cousin, Wes, was a walking encyclopedia. He could produce the most random facts yet forget the most important things, like his bike lock combination or his phone number. A week ago, he had dreaded being stuck with Wes for two months on this trip, but now his cousin was turning out to be a lot of fun and a real friend.

Soon, they entered the quaint mountain town of Buena Vista. After a couple of traffic lights, he saw a tall neon sign shaped like a giant milkshake. It read: *Old Fashioned Burgers since 1900.*

"Wow, these people have been making hamburgers for over a hundred years." Jake bent over to put his shoes on. "I hope *old-fashioned* means *gigantic* because I'm hungry."

They followed his uncle's RV into the parking lot and parked under the shade of several tall cottonwood trees, their leaves quivering in the mid-day breeze. A silver truck towing a camper pulled in behind them. It was their friends, the Catalinas, the third family joining them on the trip. Amber Catalina opened the back door of the truck and slipped on a pair of hiking boots. Her bronze skin had already grown darker during the last week in the summer sun. A streak of purple ran through her brown hair. Not bothering to tie her boots, she stuffed the laces into the tops to get them out of the way.

Wes walked out of the RV's door with his nose in a guidebook, *Exploring the Great Sand Dunes of Colorado.*

He wore a compass around his neck and a t-shirt with mountains on it that read *Take a Hike*. Several buttoned pouches and a knife sheath were snapped to his belt. As usual, his red afro was a wild mess, but it somehow looked like it had been styled that way on purpose.

"Hey, Wes, watch out!" Jake yelled.

Wes froze, then looked up from his book and saw the lip of the sidewalk. One more step and he would have been eating concrete.

"Thanks, Jake. That was close." Wes set the guidebook down on a picnic table where the parents had gathered, and then ran to get in line with Jake and Amber.

"Guys, you won't believe what I found in the guidebook!"

Jake was studying the menu board above the tall glass windows of the hamburger stand. "What did you find?"

"There's an alligator farm near the sand dunes," Wes replied. "An alligator farm!"

"Sounds cool." While Jake was figuring out what kind of milkshake he wanted, Amber stepped up to the counter and started ordering.

Wes shook his head. "You guys are obviously more interested in lunch."

"Check this out." Jake pointed to the menu board. "They have an alligator burger."

"Really." Wes craned his neck and squinted his eyes, trying to find it.

"I'm just kidding."

Wes punched his cousin, and they both smiled.

"What's your order?" a teenage girl, perhaps a year older than Jake, called out from behind the glass.

Jake stepped up to the window. "Oh, yeah. Umm... I'll take...," he began. He was caught off guard by the girl's sparkling green eyes. "Umm..."

Amber elbowed him in the side, and Wes snickered.

"I'll have a large double-chocolate milkshake, the deluxe burger, and large fries." Jake's voice squeaked when he said, "fries." He looked at the ground and shook his head in embarrassment.

The girl yelled his order out to the kitchen, wrote something on the receipt, and gave it to him. "You're Elvis Presley."

Jake took the receipt and read what she had written: *Elvis Presley*. He looked at Wes and Amber, thoroughly confused.

"It's how they call your order," Amber explained. "Instead of giving you a number, they give you the name of a famous person."

Wes ordered, took his receipt, and read it. "Oh," he said quietly, almost to himself.

"Who did you get?" Jake asked.

"Elmo."

Jake and Amber laughed.

"I bet it's because of your red hair," Amber teased.

Wes rolled his eyes. "I bet it's because I make people happy."

"No." Jake smirked. "It's your squeaky voice."

Wes whacked him in the stomach with the back of his hand.

They walked to the sidewalk and waited for their food. A few minutes later, someone called out, "Amelia Earhart!" over the loudspeaker. Amber went to the counter and picked up a red plastic tray with her burger, shake, and fried pickles.

The same voice then announced, "Elmo and Elvis Presley!"

Wes and Jake picked up their orders, and they all walked back to the picnic table and sat down in the shade of the cottonwoods.

"I was reading more about the alligator farm in that guidebook." Wes patted the book he had left on the table. "They even have gator wrestling classes. And guess what you get if you complete the class?"

"I have no idea." Jake shrugged. "A baby alligator?"

"Don't be silly." Wes shook his head. "You get a Certificate of Insanity!"

Amber was flipping through the book while she ate her fries. "Or we could visit the UFO watchtower."

"Are you serious?" He leaned over, trying to see the picture of the tower in the book. "Is that near the sand dunes, too?"

"Sure is," Wes said. "There are no city lights, so lots of people go there to see the stars and look for UFOs."

"Even if we don't go to the watchtower," Amber said, "we should definitely go out on the dunes one night and watch for shooting stars."

"Definitely." Jake nodded, then noticed that Wes had been scanning the parking lot. "Wes, what are you doing?"

"I'm keeping an eye out for those guys." He took a big slurp of his milkshake.

Amber looked back over her shoulder. "Do you think we're being followed?"

"I've been watching out the back of the RV," Wes said. "But I haven't seen any cars tailing us."

"I think we lost them when we left Twin Owls yesterday," Jake said, scanning the parking lot.

"How do you think they knew we would be at the Twin Owls?" Wes asked.

"I've been thinking about that a lot." Jake shook his head. "And I have no idea."

"Well, I'm going to be keeping an eye out." Wes

covered his mouth while he talked and chewed at the same time. "Think of me as our Head of Security."

Jake and Amber laughed.

"I'm serious," Wes stated, his voice tinged with frustration. "Those guys were after the journal. We've got to be alert."

"You're right." Jake grabbed a napkin and wiped ketchup from the corner of his mouth. "From now on, we shouldn't take the journal or scrapbook or any of the other stuff out of the camper."

"Before we left Idaho, my dad got security equipment installed," Wes pointed to his family's RV. "Once we're at the campsite, I'll aim the cameras so that they cover your camper. If anyone comes around while we're gone, we'll know."

Jake took the lid off his milkshake and began eating it with a plastic spoon. He looked up at Amber and Wes. "I found the next clue."

They both stopped chewing and stared at him.

Amber set down her burger and rested her hands, palms up, on the table. "Why didn't you tell us when we were in line?"

"It didn't feel safe." Jake looked over at a group of kids playing soccer in the park next to the hamburger stand. "I wanted to wait until it was just us." He paused, making eye contact with each of them. "It's a riddle."

"I *love* riddles!" Excitement filled Wes's eyes, and he hit the tabletop so hard their trays bounced. Jake grabbed his milkshake to keep it from toppling over.

"Our parents are still ordering," Amber said, looking at the hamburger stand. "If we hurry up and eat, we'd have time to work on the clue in your camper."

"Good idea," Jake replied. "Then let's hurry."

"Speaking of riddles," Wes interjected, "I've got one. See if you can figure *this* out: I can build castles and shrink a mountain's height; I can blind men and women and grant others their sight."

Jake and Amber thought about it for a while.

"We give up." Jake shrugged his shoulders.

"The answer is..." Wes began.

"No," Amber interrupted, "I want to figure it out." She paused to think, holding her forefinger to the side of her head. "Okay, what can shrink a mountain?"

"A glacier?" Jake offered.

"Nope," Wes said. "But you're on the right track. It's something in nature."

"Could you give us a clue?" Jake asked.

"Sure. Think about where we're going." Wes tapped his finger on the guidebook.

"The sand dunes," Jake answered.

"That's it." Amber leaned across the table. "The answer is *sand!*"

Jake was still confused. "I get the castle part because you can build a sandcastle out of sand." He rubbed his chin. "And I understand how getting sand in your eyes can blind you, but how can sand help someone see?"

Amber's furrowed eyebrows rose. "Glass! Glass is sand that's been melted down and chemically transformed." She pointed at Wes. "And eyeglasses help people see."

Wes started to say something, but Jake jumped in. "Wait, I think I've got the missing part: sand can shrink mountains by wearing them down."

"You got it. Erosion." Wes leaned back. "Now see if you can figure *this* next one out: How can you make a fire with a single stick?"

Jake thought about it for a moment. "Break it in half and rub the two sticks against each other?"

"Nope."

"I have no idea." Amber shook her head.

"Use a *matchstick*." Wes grinned.

Jake sighed. "That was so obvious!"

"Obviously, it wasn't *obvious* enough," Wes said, delight radiating from his face.

They got up, returned their trays to the window at the hamburger stand, and headed to Jake's camper. He unlocked and opened the door. Before sitting down at the table, he lifted one of the hinged bench seats to reveal a storage compartment. From under a pile of jackets and other gear, he pulled out the big leather scrapbook and a small rusty box. He closed the compartment. While Amber and Wes slid into the bench seat across from him, Jake pulled a folded envelope from his back pocket and opened it. "It's from my grandpa."

Wes shook his head, and his mouth fell open. "Wait, but your grandpa is…"

Jake could tell that Wes felt too uncomfortable to say it.

"Yeah, he's…dead." The bottom of Jake's stomach clenched when he said the word. Amber and Wes stared at the table.

He waited until their eyes rose to meet his before continuing. "It's actually kinda cool. It's the letter that the campground attendant delivered this morning before we left Rocky Mountain National Park. It's future mail."

"It's what?" Wes leaned in.

"It's a letter sent months ago by my grandpa, but with instructions to be delivered on a future date—see." He handed Wes the envelope. A sticker on the front read: *Deliver on June 2nd, 2019.*"

Before his grandpa passed away, he had planned this trip for Jake's family, creating their itinerary and booking their campsites. He knew Jake's parents intended to honor his wishes and his memory by taking that trip. Because of this, he knew where Jake would be during the two months they were visiting the national parks.

"I'll skip the first part of the letter, but here's the clue." Jake read it out loud."

Jax,

I hope that you've found the journal by now. However, if you haven't, you've got plenty of time—an entire lifetime—to return and search for it. If you did find it, be sure to keep it hidden. We've reason to believe that it's valuable, and that there are others who are looking for it. This quest, I suppose, is much bigger than either you or I understand. With love,

Grandpa

PS: Your Next Clue
Click, Click, Click, Click, Click, Click.
They become visible in the dark.
Assemble the vista.
And look for the mark.

He set the letter down on the table and raised his eyebrows. "What do you think?"

Wes bunched his lips together and tapped on the table six times. "Maybe it's morse code, like the clue you found in the scrapbook—the one that led us to Emerald Lake."

"What do six clicks mean in morse code?" Amber looked at Wes, expecting him to know.

Wes held up six fingers. "Six means *six*."

"Six what?" Jake asked.

"Six dashes in morse code just means the *number* six." Wes shrugged and lifted his hands. "That's all it means."

"How about the next part?" Jake ran his fingers along the second line of the note as he read it. "*They become visible in the dark.*"

Amber closed her eyes and took in a deep breath. She opened them again. "Maybe stars? You can only see them at night."

"I bet that's it." Jake looked at the ceiling, scanning his brain to find a connection. "Maybe... it's six stars."

"Lyra!" Wes half jumped out of his seat. "It's a constellation with *six* stars!"

"How do you know stuff like that?" Amber shook her head.

"I just do." Wes shrugged. "Anyway, Lyra is supposed to look like a harp."

"Okay," Jake muttered. "Let's keep thinking about it. It could be that constellation, but it might be something else."

Wes turned the paper so that he and Amber could read it. She mouthed the words: *Assemble the vista*, then looked up at Jake. "Open the scrapbook and find the sand dunes."

Jake pulled the scrapbook from across the table and turned its pages. There were pictures of waterfalls and old keepsake stamps from different national parks. One sheet contained a single photo of the Grand Canyon that filled the entire page. Then he came to the Great Sand Dunes, where two pages were filled with black and white photographs of vast wind-shaped mountains of sand. In one photo, a man walked alone in the distance, almost a speck against the massive landscape. He turned the scrapbook around and pushed it across the table to Amber.

She gently tapped each photo and counted, "One, two, three, four, five, six."

Jake leaned forward and blinked his eyes. "The click. It's a camera. It's the sound a camera makes when you take a picture. Six clicks mean *six photos*."

Amber nodded. "And they become visible in the dark."

Jake narrowed his eyes, confused. "Do you mean they are like glow-in-the-dark or something?"

"Ohhh!" Wes sat up straight. "I get it!" He looked at Amber. "Can I say it?"

She nodded.

"Old photos like this, they had to expose in a dark room." Wes stared at one of the photographs. "At first, the film was just white, but when they put it in chemicals, the picture would slowly develop."

Jake looked across the table at Wes and whispered, "*They become visible in the dark.*"

Wes nodded and smiled at his cousin.

"I've got an idea," Amber said, laying her finger on the scrapbook. "Could you take the pictures out?"

Jake carefully slid the first photograph out of its triangular mounts. Before placing it on the table, he flipped it over to see if anything was written on the back. This is how he found the first clue in Rocky Mountain National Park. But this time, there was nothing. He did the same with the other five photos. Again, nothing.

They passed the six photos around. Then Amber gently took one of the photographs out of Wes's hand. He glared at her but soon became interested in what she was doing. She placed the photo alongside another one. Together, they created one big picture. "I think they form a panorama," she explained. As she arranged the others, the six photos came to create a single large picture. The Great Sand Dunes were in the middle, the mountains behind, and a shallow, sandy creek filled the foreground.

"That's it," Wes exclaimed. "The riddle told us to *assemble* the vista."

Just then, the camper door opened, and Jake's mom poked her head in. "Hey guys, we're going to leave in five minutes."

"Thanks, Mrs. Evans," Amber replied.

"Yeah, thanks, Mom." Jake didn't take his eyes off the puzzle Amber had fitted together.

As the door swung shut, its glass caught the light of the sun, throwing a glare across the photos. At that instant, Jake saw it. The photos had a sheen to them, but some spots were dull, and those muted areas looked like they might be letters. "Look for the mark," he murmured, and then he looked up at Amber. "Could I borrow your phone for a second?"

"Sure." She pulled her phone out of her back pocket and handed it to Jake, who turned on the flashlight and passed its beam over the landscape.

"You've got to be kidding me!" Wes exclaimed. "There are words on there!"

"I'm going to try something." He switched on the camera app, turned on the flash, and took a picture. His idea worked. The flash made the glossy parts stand out from the dull areas, revealing the clue. He set the phone on the table, and they all stared at the message.

Wes read it out loud: *Elmyra Holcomb.*

Jake squinted and drew closer to the letters to make sure Wes had read them correctly. He was right. The letters spelled: *Elmyra Holcomb."*

"Sounds like a name," Amber offered. "A really old name."

Jake shined the light across the lower half of the

photos. "There's more." He held the light still and read: "*Caverna...Del...Oro*? Sounds like Spanish."

Wes looked at Amber. "You're Spanish. Can you read that?"

She gave Wes a shove. "I'm *not* Spanish. I'm Argentine."

"Sorry." Wes cringed at his mistake. "So, can you read it?" he asked again.

"Yeah, I can," Amber replied. "*Caverna Del Oro* means...the *Cavern of Gold*."

CHAPTER 3

THE GREAT SAND DUNES

The families drove south toward the sand dunes. About an hour later, they passed the Colorado Gators Reptile Park. Then, they turned left onto a country road that stretched for miles and appeared to lead to nowhere. Jake could see a brown haze against the distant mountains, and it grew larger with every passing mile.

"Are those the sand dunes?" he asked.

"They sure are," his dad replied.

Jake noticed movement in the passenger-side mirror and watched as Uncle Brian and Aunt Judy's RV pulled off the road with their jeep in tow behind them. "Where is Uncle Brian going?" he asked.

"He needed to get a few supplies," Jake's mom

answered, "and he volunteered to pick up some sand-boards for you guys."

"That's so cool!" Jake replied.

"You kids can repay us by doing all the dishes and keeping camp in order." His dad's mouth betrayed a very slight smile.

Jake sighed. His parents had endless creative ways to assign chores on this trip. "I thought this was a vacation."

"There is no vacation from chores," his dad answered.

The truck hit a dip, jerked, and the tires made a loud rumble. Jake grabbed the seat in front of him to steady himself. "What in the world was that? I mean, someone put that thing right in the middle of the road!"

"It's a cattle guard," his mom replied. "The cows out here graze in large areas that have roads running through them. Instead of putting gates across the roads, the farmers dig trenches and lay metal grates into the ground."

"That stops the cows from getting out?" Jake asked.

"It does," his mom replied. "To a cow, it looks like a dark pit, so they won't try crossing it."

Sure enough, only a couple of miles down the road, a herd of cattle crossed in front of them. Several of the animals stood on the asphalt, chewing grass they had pulled from the roadside. Jake's dad slowed down, and eventually, the cows moved aside, letting him through.

Soon they arrived at the park entrance, where they

stopped at a pull-off point, and the families took pictures of one another in front of the large sign that read: *Great Sand Dunes National Park and Preserve*. From here, the dunes were no longer a sand-colored blur on the horizon but tall hills with twisting ridgelines. Behind the dunes stood the green flanks of the Sangre De Cristo Mountains, and Mount Herard towered above them, its peak still covered in early summer snow. Winds on the mountaintop blew spindrift into the air. Jake had never in his life seen anything like this.

They all made their way past the visitor center to the Piñon Flats campground, where Amber and Jake set up camp while they waited for Wes's family to arrive. They found spots to hang the hammocks, set the camp chairs around the fire, and walked down to the camp store to buy firewood.

When they were almost back at their campsite, the plastic strap on Jake's bundle of logs came loose, and his firewood crashed onto the road. An older man sitting under the awning of his camper got up from his lawn chair and walked over to help.

"Thank you, sir," Jake said to the man, who was reaching down to pick up a log.

"You're welcome. Where are you kids from?" The man's thick, brown and gray mustache covered his upper lip as he talked. He picked up another log and cinched down the flat cap he wore—the kind Jake had seen golfers wear—so that it would not slip from his head.

"I'm from California," Amber replied.

"And our family is from Ohio," Jake added.

"You're from our neck of the woods then." His friendliness and the creases around his eyes reminded Jake of his grandfather. But the unusual color of the man's smokey gray eyes is what most caught his attention.

"My wife, Bonnie, and I are from just north of Pittsburgh. I'm Gus."

"I'm Jake, and this is Amber."

Just then, the RV drove by with Wes waving at them through the back window.

"And I guess that red-headed young man is with you two?" Gus raised an eyebrow.

"Yeah, that's my cousin, Wes. He's kinda crazy."

"Are you staying for a while?" Gus asked.

"We are," Amber replied. "We have three days here, but we're going to a bunch of parks over the next couple of months."

"We do the same thing every summer." Gus picked up the last piece of the fallen firewood. "Where are you headed next?"

"The Grand Canyon," Jake replied.

"You guys are going to love it," Gus said. "And maybe we'll see you there, too. That's also our next stop."

Gus helped them carry the loose logs back to the campsite. While Gus introduced himself to their parents, Amber and Jake ran over to meet Wes, who was getting out of the RV, carrying what looked like two plywood snowboards. "Can you believe this place? I mean, I feel like we just stepped onto the moon!" Wes spun around to take in the landscape, almost hitting Jake in the head with one of the boards.

"Be careful, Wes. You almost took my head off."

"Sorry, Jake." He handed each of them a board. "These are the sandboards. My dad said that once we get camp set up, we can go try them out on the dunes."

Jake and Amber hurried to help Wes get things

settled; then, they all went to change into clothes better suited for crossing the creek and boarding the dunes. They packed water and snacks into their daypacks, put the sandboards over their shoulders, and began their hike toward the sand dunes. But to get there, they first had to cross Medano Creek. It was early June, and that meant the snowfields in the nearby mountains were melting, creating rivulets in the high country that twisted and turned their way down into the creeks, which dropped through gorges, gulches, and canyons and flowed into the irrigation ditches dug into the plains of the San Luis Valley.

But no other mountain stream was like Medano Creek. Its waters cut through the sand flats at the base of the dunes, where it widens to the span of a football field. As it flows downhill, the Medano piles up heaps of wet sand. Hidden under the water, these invisible dams grow until they collapse under the building pressure, sending surge waves rolling through the sandy, shallow creek.

Jake scanned the broad stretch of sand and water. Families lined the banks and even more were scattered throughout its shallow waters, laughing and playing in the wet sand.

"This is weird," Wes said, surveying the landscape. "It's like we're at the beach!"

"I know." Jake shook his head in amazement. "I

thought this was going to be the kind of creek you just jump over. But it's huge!"

They took off their shoes and socks, put them in their packs, and began walking across the creekbed. The cool, wet sand felt spongy under their feet. Soon, the water was up to their knees, and when the wet sandy mud surged under their feet, Jake was the first to fall. Like a domino, he toppled into Amber, who collided with Wes, who landed face down in the sand. He worked to get up, spitting the watery sand out of his mouth.

"What just happened?" Wes asked.

"I don't know," Jake replied. "It was like the ground caved in under my feet."

"Check this out, guys!" Amber said, pointing upstream to where another surge had just broken loose, sending a wave directly at them. Jake and Wes immediately sat down beside her just in time to feel the cool wave splash across their chests. They laughed as they watched the sand collapse in different places around them, sometimes creating cascades, and other times more waves. Little kids with inflatable pool floats went drifting by them. Other kids covered themselves head to toe with the mud-like sand, then sat down in the Medano to wash it all away.

Amber stood up with her sandboard. In her other hand was a giant glob of wet sand. She dropped it on top of Jake's head, then ran upstream as fast as she could.

Surprised and laughing, Jake grabbed two handfuls of the grainy slush and pursued her, pelting her legs.

Arriving at the edge of the creek, she found a safe spot for her things, which had somehow been spared from getting soaked. Gathering more sludge in her hands, she launched a fresh assault on Jake.

"Ouch!" he yelled as a glob splattered across his chest. "That one really stung!" He was caught off guard when Wes hit him from behind with another giant sandball. Amber came at him, howling with laughter, her hands full of sludge. All Jake could do was crouch down in the shallow water and shield his head from the onslaught. It was two against one, and he was soon completely covered in the wet, brown sand.

"I give up! I give up!" he yelled as he slowly rose to his feet and raised his hands in the air. Amber walked up and gave him a shove. Jake fell back into the creek, laughing. Wes and Amber joined him, and they all worked to wash the grit and grime from their skin and clothes.

Then Jake realized that two of the sandboards were gone, drifting downstream with the current. Wes spotted them, too. In a flash, he jumped up and sprinted after them.

Jake helped Amber to her feet. Then he went to help Wes recover their boards.

Slogging their way out of the creek, the kids made their

way to where Amber had stashed her things along its banks at the foot of the dunes. She opened her pack and then breathed a sigh of relief. "I completely forgot about my phone. But everything is pretty much dry."

The boy's backpacks hadn't faired as well. They sat down beside her, took out their wet socks and shoes, and put them on over their sandy feet.

Wes was the first to stand. "We should get moving if we want to ride the boards."

Jake and Amber finished tying their shoes and grabbed their boards. Climbing the first dune, they soon realized just how difficult it would be to hike to the top. Amber was in the lead, but the going was slow. "Every time I step forward, I slip back," she complained.

"I know," Wes replied. "At this rate, it's going to take forever to get to the top."

Jake looked up to see that the top of the dune was now hidden by the steep hill of sand they were climbing. "What time are we supposed to be back?" he asked.

"My mom said dinnertime," Amber answered.

"It sure feels like dinnertime already," Wes grumbled. "This climb is making me hungry."

They trudged their way to the top of the first dune and turned around to look down on the creek and out to the mountains that stretched into the south. They could see the now distant campground and the tiny, moving figures of people in the creek. Turning back to the north, they looked across the dunefield. It was like being dropped into a vast desert landscape.

"See up there, where those people are?" Jake pointed to the highest dune on the horizon. "Let's see if we can get up there, then board our way back down."

"I think that's farther than it looks," Amber said. "But I'm up for it."

Wes nodded in agreement while chewing on a beef stick he had pulled from his pack. "But we should hurry up. It's six o'clock already."

About thirty minutes later, they were walking the ridge of the big dune, just below its summit. All the people they had seen at the top were now walking back. One hiker they passed told them that they were on High Dune, the second-highest peak in the park.

When they got to the top, the sky was turning a deep blue, and the clouds were shifting from white to pink. "Guys, I'm seeing something kinda weird." Wes tried to use his hand to shield his eyes from the light of the westering sun.

"What is it?" Jake asked. He followed Wes's eye-line to a spot in the west.

"Down there." Wes pointed below them. "It's like a mirage. I mean, it looks like a lake in the middle of the dunes."

Amber unzipped her backpack and pulled out the map she'd picked up at the visitor center, "There aren't any lakes in the dunes—see." She showed them the map. The closest blue mark on it was over four miles away, and the other blue circles that indicated ponds and small lakes were even further.

"What if we board down to it?" Wes asked.

Before they could discuss it, Wes had strapped on his sandboard and was flying down the side of High Dune toward the gleam of water.

CHAPTER 4

THIEVES

J ake and Amber strapped on their boards and shot down the mountain of sand, cutting long arches across its slopes.

"Amber, you're really good!" Jake yelled across to her as she passed.

"It's just like snowboarding," she called back.

They pursued Wes, who was cutting back and forth through the sand below them. He slowed at the crest of another dune, then disappeared over its edge. Seconds later, Amber vanished over the rim. When Jake reached the same spot on the dune's edge, he looked down to discover that it was a good thing he had stopped. The slip face of the dune was almost a straight drop-off. Amber and Wes had both wiped out and were dusting themselves off, groaning as they inspected the angry-red sandpaper scratches on their arms and legs.

"Take it slow!" Amber yelled up.

"Yeah, *we* found out the hard way," Wes added.

Jake dropped over the edge and boarded down to them. They were at the rim of yet another dune. Amber made her way to look over the edge.

"Hey...guys... we're there," she panted, catching her breath.

Wes and Jake picked up their boards and walked over. Below them, in what looked like a crater of smooth sand, was a pond the size of a tennis court. Its water was clear all the way to the bottom, and the pink and orange sky reflected on its surface. Scanning the area and the dunes behind them, they could see the place was deserted.

After boarding down into the pit, they unstrapped and approached the pond. Near the edge of the water, Jake's foot hit something. He bent down and brushed the sand away from the object. Soon a broken piece of old pottery began to appear. "Hey, guys, check this out!"

Amber and Wes joined him, and they all dug away at the sand until they unearthed the remains of a large bowl painted with intricate patterns.

"What the heck?" Wes exclaimed. "How did this get here?"

"Hey, guys," Amber called out. "There's more." She

knelt at the edge of the pond, staring into the water. "I think those are bones."

Wes's eyes got huge. "You mean...human bones?"

"I can't tell," she said, "but those are definitely bones of some kind."

The partial remains of a rib cage lay in the water, the tips of its white, curved shape sticking out from the surface of the pond.

"There's all kinds of stuff in there." Wes stared into the water. "I'm going in." He took off his shoes and waded toward the middle. The water was shallow, reaching only to the bottom of his shorts. He bent over and pulled something from the bed of the pond.

"What is it?" Jake asked.

Wes held up a long, cylindrical stone. "I have no idea," he said, turning the object over in his hand. "But it looks man-made because it's so smooth." He washed it off in the water and handed it to Jake.

"This is amazing," Jake breathed. "But something doesn't feel right."

Amber nodded. "Yeah, I've got the same feeling, like we're not supposed to be messing with this stuff."

"It reminds me of Mesa Verde," said Wes.

"What do you mean?" Jake asked.

"Well, a long time ago, before Mesa Verde was a national park, a bunch of people went in there and took artifacts like this. And now a lot of them are lost —forever."

Jake carefully set the polished stone back on the ground near the water's edge. He could smell the metallic scent of the pond. He stood up and looked around. Surrounded by walls of sand, the world had become silent.

"I've got an idea." Amber reached into her pack and pulled out her phone. She took a picture of the pond, the stone cylinder, the bones, and the decorative pot. "Let's go tell the rangers and show them the photos."

They gathered their sandboards and began their journey back to camp. At the ridge of the first dune, Wes stopped to look back at the sunset. "Hey, guys, come back. There's something you need to see."

Jake and Amber had begun to walk back to where Wes stood, when suddenly he dropped to the ground. "Guys, get down. Now!"

"Why?" Jake asked.

"Just do it!" Wes whispered. "Quick!"

Jake and Amber dropped to the sand and began army crawling to where Wes lay at the lip of the dune. When they reached him, they could see why he had been acting so strangely. Far below them, three figures were making their way down the opposite dune toward the water. They had large, tan backpacks, which they set down at the water's edge. From the packs, they each pulled large, blue, waterproof bags; the kind raft guides used to pack their gear. Two of the figures began wading out into the pond.

"Guys," Amber said, her voice wary, "Something feels really weird about this."

Wes drew a set of small binoculars out of his pack, looked through them for a moment, then passed them to Jake. With the binoculars, he could see more clearly. One of the backpackers, a young woman wearing a black ball cap, pulled something out of the water and was carrying it back to the sand. A young man wearing cargo pants was picking artifacts from the edge of the water, drying them on his green shirt, and stuffing them into one of the vinyl bags.

Jake then spied the third guy. He was in the middle of the pond, pulling up some of the bones and dragging them toward the packs. He appeared older than the other two, wore his long hair in a ponytail, and a broad-rimmed hat set atop his head.

The sun was quickly disappearing behind the western range of mountains, turning the figures below into dark silhouettes. He passed the binoculars to Amber.

After examining the scene, she whispered, "We've got to get back *fast* and tell the rangers."

"Yeah," Jake agreed, "this is no good at all. It's like you said about Mesa Verde, Wes—how people would just come and take the artifacts."

"I'm pretty sure it's totally illegal," Amber said.

Jake turned to Amber. "Can your phone get a signal?"

Just then, a patch of sand along the rim broke loose from under Wes's elbows and slid down the face of the dune. The three kids scrambled back from the edge. Below them, the figures froze and peered up at the top of the dune. Jake, Amber, and Wes tried to melt into the sand, where they waited and listened in silence.

Slowly, Amber drew the phone out of her back pocket and checked for a signal.

"No service."

"Okay," Jake replied, "I'm going to check to see if they saw us." He slinked forward and peeked over the edge. The three thieves were already back at work. One had unearthed the pottery Jake found earlier, and the others were using shovels to dig out things below the surface. They packed each one carefully into the bags.

"They didn't see us," he exhaled with relief. "What if we use the beacon?"

In Rocky Mountain National Park, before their parents had allowed them to hike alone, they'd been given an emergency beacon. Instead of relying on cell towers for service, the device communicated with satellites to send a distress signal and their location to their parents and local authorities.

Wes pressed his forehead into the sand and sighed. Then he looked back up. "I didn't bring it."

"Don't worry. Most of the trip back is downhill," Amber explained. "With the boards, I bet we can make it back in less than an hour."

"We're going to have to fly," Jake said.

They crawled back until they could safely stand up without being seen, grabbed their boards, and sprinted across the sand. In the distance, they could still see lights and fires at the Piñon Flats campground. As they boarded and ran back to camp, their purple shadows rippled across the smooth contours of the dunes, now lit red by the last rays of the setting sun.

CHAPTER 5

1880 - THE DESCENT

"I'll be right back, boy." Emma gently touched the dog's forehead. She got up and ran to Gideon, whose ears were perked and turned toward the baying of the hounds coming from the ridge above the lake.

"Gideon, there's someone we've got to help." She untied the horse's reins from the tree and led him into the thicket. There, she invited him to sniff the dog while she stroked her horse's muzzle. "He's our friend, and he's in trouble." Gideon flared his nostrils and nodded his head.

Emma bent down, slipped her arms under the dog, and hoisted him onto the front of Gideon's saddle. Exhausted and limp, the retriever didn't protest. She opened the saddlebag and found a couple of long leather straps. After climbing into the saddle, she laced the straps around the dog to secure him for the ride. The barks and howls were getting closer.

Emma leaned over to speak into Gideon's ear. "We can't take the straight path home, boy. They'll follow us too easily. We'll have to find our own way down the mountain." She guided her horse into the forest. Fallen trees crisscrossed the landscape. Thick brush and saplings crowded out any possibility of an easy descent. But this was exactly what she wanted. If the hounds had chased this poor animal to the point of collapse, then they must be weary, too. This tangled forest floor would slow their pursuit.

The girl, horse, and dog went carefully into gullies, over logs, and through steep slick patches of snow. After nearly a mile of working their way down the mountainside, Emma stopped Gideon, got down, and fed her horse a handful of oats from the saddlebag. After eating his snack, Gideon drank from a puddle of snowmelt. She offered the dog a piece of dried beef. He licked at its salty surface but refused to eat. Knowing this wasn't a good sign, Emma's concern heightened. She cupped her hands to draw water from the puddle and brought it to the dog's mouth. He lapped at the water.

She went back to the puddle to scoop another handful. Just as she went to give the dog a second drink, he startled and whined. She looked at Gideon, who had turned his head to look back into the forest. Though Emma heard nothing, she trusted the senses of her companions. She also knew that the scent of a horse like Gideon's was strong and easy to follow. By now, the hounds had certainly connected his scent with the scent of the dog.

She climbed back into the saddle, and they continued their struggle through the wild and jumbled forest floor.

"Gideon, we're going to have to go through Hatchet Gash."

He let out a low snort through his nostrils.

"I know, boy. It's the last place you'd want to go. But I don't think we've got a choice now."

CHAPTER 6

MIDNIGHT AT THE LIBERTY GATE

Jake, Wes, and Amber raced down the last slope into the broad sand plain that marked the end of the dunes. They could see the lights of Piñon Flats campground on the other side of the creek. It was almost dark, with a few stars now visible in the deep blue eastern sky, and the creek shimmered like silver in the twilight. Unstrapping from his sandboard, Jake noticed a lone hiker crossing Medano Creek.

The man continued walking in their direction. As he got closer, Jake noticed that he looked familiar. It was Gus, their neighbor at the campground. Gus waved and yelled something the kids couldn't discern. They threw their boards over their shoulders and sprinted toward him. When they reached him, they were completely winded.

"Are you guys all okay?" Gus asked.

"We are," Jake said, still trying to catch his breath.

"Your parents were getting concerned. So, I told them I'd come out here and scan the dunes for you."

"We found a pond...in the dunes," Jake explained. "And some old pottery...and bones and stuff."

"Wow!" Gus slid his hands into his pockets. "That's quite a find. I'm sure the park service will want to know about this."

"Yeah, but it's not good," Wes added, slowly shaking his head. "Some people came, and they're out there taking all the stuff."

Gus's eyebrows tightened, the look of concern making his features sharp, almost angry. "I'll tell you what, you kids head back to your parents just as fast as you can, and I'll walk down to the headquarters and find a ranger."

"Okay. Thanks, Gus," Jake replied.

They crossed the creek without stopping to take off their shoes and socks and then ran across the road and up the trail that led into the campground. Their parents had lit a fire and were cleaning up what remained of dinner.

"What happened to you guys?" Mrs. Evan's hands rested on her hips as she surveyed the long red scrapes on Jake's arms and the sand covering all their shoes and legs. "We were starting to get *really* worried." He could tell by the tone of his mom's voice that she was more upset than she let on.

"Mom, I'm sorry we're so late, but we found something."

His mom looked confused.

Amber pulled out her phone, opened the photos app, and handed it to Jake's mom. "We discovered this pond in the middle of the sand dunes. And all these artifacts."

The other parents gathered around them to look at the photos.

"We wanted to rush back here and tell a Ranger," Wes added. "But when we were leaving, these three people showed up at the pond." His face grew serious. "And they started *taking* the stuff."

"They didn't see us," Amber added. "And I tried to call you guys, but we couldn't get a phone signal."

Mr. Catalina looked from the photos to the kids. "Did you see Mr. Teller? He went out to look for you guys."

"We saw him." Jake nodded. "He went to tell a ranger."

Just then, a green truck pulled up beside their campsite. Gus slid out of the passenger side. Leaving his truck's engine running, a park ranger got out and walked over. He wore a straight-brimmed hat that made him look even taller than he was. His gray mustache grew along the sides of his mouth, reminding Jake of a sheriff from an old Western movie. The gold badge on his gray-pocketed shirt gleamed in the flickering light of the campfire.

"Hi, kids, I'm Ranger Trujillo." He reached out to shake each of their hands. "Sounds like you three have had an eventful afternoon. Mr. Teller here says you kids stumbled onto something in the dunes and that there might be a situation we need to look into."

Amber was the first to answer. "We found a pond and some things around it." She handed the ranger her phone. Its light illuminated his face as he swiped through the pictures.

"And then we saw three people start digging up all the stuff and taking it," Jake said.

Ranger Trujillo pulled at his green tie, and his face went from curious to serious. "Please, excuse me for a moment." He walked to the truck and grabbed his radio. "I need someone posted ASAP to monitor the Dunes Lot and someone at the Liberty Gate Trailhead. I'll get you more information just as soon as I have it." He clipped the radio onto his belt and walked back to the campsite.

"I know it's getting late, folks, but I'm wondering if one of the kids and a parent could join me. I need to make a patrol of the area, and if we find the looters, I'll need someone to identify them."

"Could we all three come?" Jake asked. "I mean, if you have enough room."

Wes and Amber turned to see how their parents would respond.

"It's fine with me," Aunt Judy said. "But you kids need to get some food in you before you leave."

"Sounds like a good way to get out of dish duty to me," Uncle Brian said, a smirk on his face. "But seriously, I'd like to ride along with you all."

Amber looked at her parents, who both nodded in approval.

"I'll let you three eat your dinner, and I'll be back to pick you up in about twenty minutes." Ranger Trujillo turned to walk back to his truck. "Bring some snacks," he called back, "and water because we'll be out late—probably until early morning."

Jake, Wes, and Amber scarfed down dinner and filled their water bottles. They packed some cheese sticks, fruit leather, trail mix, and some chocolate milk into a small cooler, enough to supply them with the energy they'd need to get through the night. When Ranger Trujillo arrived, they loaded into the back seat of the truck, and Uncle Brian got into the front passenger seat.

Wes fastened his seatbelt, then clapped his hands together. "So, where are we going?"

Ranger Trujillo looked over his shoulder as he backed up the truck. "The most likely place the looters would've parked is up north, at the Liberty Gate."

He shifted the truck from reverse into drive. "It's only ten miles from here as the crow flies, but there are no roads through the dunes. We're going to have to drive around the park; it's going to be a *long* trip. But I've got plenty of questions for you three, so I'm sure the time will pass quickly. How about you start by describing the looters?"

"There were two guys and one girl," Jake said. "And they were young. Like my brother Nick's age. He's in college."

"They were wearing hiking stuff," Amber added. "And had big backpacks, like they were going on a camping trip. But...the packs looked mostly empty."

"Tell me more about what they were wearing."

Amber sighed. "I wish that I had taken a picture, but I was afraid they'd see us."

Wes leaned forward and put his head between the front seats. "I remember that the girl had on a black ball cap with some kind of green symbol. She had blond hair... in pigtails." He scratched his chin. "Oh, yeah, and one of the guys had long, brown hair—like the same length as the girl's hair—and he was wearing a blue hat. It was kinda funny-looking, like a sun hat. The other guy was the tallest and had a short beard. He was wearing those pants with a bunch of pockets. And I think his shirt was green."

Jake gently elbowed his cousin and whispered, "Impressive memory."

"Is there anything else that stood out to you?" Ranger Trujillo asked.

All three of them pondered for a moment. "I don't think so," Jake replied. "It was starting to get dark, so it was hard to see."

"Oh, I know," Amber said. "All their backpacks were the same."

"Yeah," Wes added. "They were tan, with a camo-print on them, like you see people in the army use."

"Oh, and remember?" Jake turned to Wes and Amber. "They had these glossy blue bags, too. That's what they were putting the artifacts into."

Ranger Trujillo picked up his radio. Its red lights reflected off the inside of the windshield. He pressed the button and repeated the descriptions of the looters to someone on the other end. He sat the radio on the console in between the front seats and then turned to Uncle Brian. "I see you're wearing a John Deere hat. Do you farm?"

Uncle Brian touched the brim of his hat and nodded. "Yep. Growing up in Indiana, our family raised cattle and farmed about four hundred acres. I'm an engineer now, but we have a small hobby farm in Idaho. We keep a garden and raise a few cows each year. How about you?"

"Yeah, my family has been here farming in the valley for several generations. It can be a hard life, but it's about as honest a living a person can make, working outside with your hands, watching and caring for things that grow." He flicked the turn signal and then rounded the truck onto a new road. "Here in the San Luis Valley, it's all about water." He glanced toward the backseat and continued, "In fact, the most surprising discovery you kids made today wasn't the artifacts. It was that little pond of water."

"We did think it was kinda unusual," Jake said. "But after finding the pottery and bones and stuff, I guess we didn't think much more about it."

"What you discovered is called an *interdunal pond*," Ranger Trujillo explained. "I've lived here all my life and never seen one—just heard about them. We have a geologist on staff, and she's been saying that with all the melting snowpack and unusual amount of rain, we might see one. It's a rare event, kinda like a comet that only comes around every hundred years."

"So, why were all the artifacts there?" Amber asked.

"Well, imagine the dunes as a bunch of yellow icebergs in a sea of sand. On the surface, you just see their tall, swirled peaks. But if you could see underneath the dunes, you'd find that the dunefield is saturated with water, making all that sand heavier and holding the whole thing in place."

"But that doesn't explain why all the artifacts were there," Wes said.

"Patience—I'm getting there," Ranger Trujillo replied. "First, you've got to understand how the dunes work for this to all make sense."

Jake leaned forward. He found the conversation mysterious and interesting.

"Like I said earlier," Ranger Trujillo continued, "these ponds only show up when there's an unusual abundance of water. But our archeologists and geologists believe that thousands of years back, this region received *a lot* more rain. Because of that, the interdunal ponds might have been something the indigenous people were used to seeing."

"Indigenous?" Jake had heard the word before, but he couldn't remember what it meant.

"That's just another word for *native*. Now, I'm talking about the *ancient* folks, what archeologists call the *Folsom* and the *Clovis* peoples. They hunted mammoths and huge extinct bison right here in this valley. In fact, just a few minutes ago, when we drove over that cattle guard, we passed by the site of an old Folsom hunting camp."

"Wow," Jake whispered. The idea of people living here thousands of years ago and encountering giant animals captivated his imagination.

"Whenever these ponds appear for us to study, folks find bones and ancient tools left by the indigenous people. Our theory is that these ponds would appear in the same spots, and the ancient tribes considered them sacred ground where they would come to camp and sometimes bury their dead."

"That's kinda strange," Wes wondered aloud. "Why would they bury people there?"

"Well, have you kids ever read the *Narnia* books?" Ranger Trujillo asked.

"Those are my absolute favorite!" Amber leaned in. All three of the kids scooted forward in their seats.

"If you remember, in the first book, Digory and Polly travel between different worlds through little pools of water. It may be that those ancient tribes saw these inter-dunal ponds in the same way, as doorways into another world."

"Whoa," Wes whispered.

"So, the theory is they wanted to bury their loved ones and leaders near that entrance to the afterlife."

Ranger Trujillo made a right-hand turn off the highway onto a paved county road. He pulled a toothpick out of a container and placed it between his teeth. It was the flavored kind, and it filled the cab with the smell of cinnamon. Though it was night, Jake could see the moonlit peaks of the Sangre De Cristo Mountains in the east. His mind wandered. He had always imagined sand dunes in remote deserts far away in Africa or in the middle of Saudi Arabia, not in the middle of the Rocky Mountains. He decided to ask Ranger Trujillo about it. "Mr. Trujillo, how did the dunes get here?"

"Can you picture in your mind one of those recycling

symbols? You know, the one with the three green arrows going in a circle?"

"Yeah," Jake replied.

"Now, in your mind, bend the points of those arrows inward so they all point toward the center. And imagine that symbol over the top of a map of the Great Sand Dunes."

"One of those arrows represents the wind, bringing sand through the air from the San Juan Mountains, over sixty miles southwest from here. There's evidence that over thousands of years that blowing sand accumulated in the bowl of a huge lake located just west of here. And then, that ancient lake dried up, leaving a giant bathtub of sand. Ever since the winds have kept on blowing out of the west and piling all that dry sand into great heaps."

Jake could see it all in his mind, like a movie on fast forward: the clouds racing past, the seasons changing, streams of sand swirling into the air, and the dunes growing inch by inch and foot by foot.

"Now, imagine a second arrow coming from the opposite direction. These are the storm winds streaming down the western slopes of the Sangre De Cristo Mountains, pushing dirt and sand back down toward the dunefield. The two winds are still pushing the sands together, shaping the changing surface of the place.

"The third arrow is the water coming down out of the

mountains, soaking the sand and acting like a giant anchor, holding the whole thing in place."

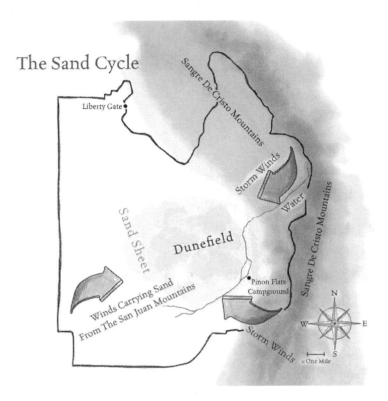

The Sand Cycle

"And all of that is still happening?" Jake asked.

"It sure is. But it's only in the last fifty years or so that we've started to understand it. In fact, there's a good chance the sand dunes could have been lost if some good people had not intervened."

"Did people want to haul away the sand or something?" Amber guessed, her words uncertain.

"Not exactly." Ranger Trujillo flipped on the truck's high beams and slowed the truck. Three whitetail deer crossed the road in front of them. Jake watched out his windows as they jumped a fence and faded into the night.

"There are traces of gold in the dunes, and there have been attempts to mine it, but all those gold operations failed. And that was a long time ago, before the sand dunes were declared a national monument. Out here in the western parts of the United States, there's something even more valuable than gold."

"More valuable than gold?" Wes sounded thoroughly confused. "Are there diamonds out here?"

"Not diamonds, Wes. *Water*."

The truck's headlight lit up a sign that read, *Welcome to Crestone, Established 1880, Elevation 8000'*. The truck continued past the small town and headed south along the foot of the mountains.

"Let me guess," Wes mused. "Someone was trying to sell the water?"

"Exactly. There were companies buying up land around the sand dunes with plans to pump the water out of the aquifers—big underground lakes—and send that water in pipelines to different cities. It all gets really complicated. But those aquifers stretch out under the dunes, and we believe they are the main element holding the dunes in place."

Wes's eyebrows knit together. "So, if they were to drain those underground lakes, the dunes might just blow away?"

"You've got it," Ranger Trujillo replied. "Now, it wouldn't happen right away, but year after year, and decade after decade, the dunes would get smaller because the cycle I described earlier would be broken. So, when the National Park was established, we worked with an organization called the Nature Conservancy to buy up the land and the water rights from those companies. Together, we were able to protect not just the dunefield, but the whole ecosystem that surrounds it, and makes that sand cycle work."

They turned onto a dirt road that was washboarded with bumps. The jostling and bouncing made their teeth chatter and their jaws vibrate inside their heads.

"Sorry, these next few miles are going to be a bit uncomfortable," Ranger Trujillo said.

The truck's headlights cut a slice of light through the darkness and dust until they entered a small parking area. Jake noticed a sheriff's truck parked beside a white, dust-covered SUV. "We're at the Liberty Gate Trailhead, and I'm guessing our looters will return to that vehicle." Ranger Trujillo pointed at the SUV. He parked the truck and dimmed the headlights. "I'm going to talk with Sheriff Beyers. I'll be back in a moment."

Wes turned on the cab light above him and opened his map of the sand dunes.

"What are you doing, Wes?" his dad asked.

"I'm trying to figure out how long it would take the looters to hike from the pond to here." He turned the map around until he found what he was looking for. "Does anyone have a pen I can borrow?"

Amber pulled one out of her pack and handed it to him. Beginning at High Dune, Wes put a dash on the map for every mile between it and the Liberty Gate. "So, if they hiked straight here from High Dune—which is the closest thing on the map to the pond—that would be about twelve miles."

"Wow, that's a long haul." Jake stared down at the marks Wes had drawn on the map.

"Their path won't take them in a straight line, though," Uncle Brian said. "So, you're going to want to add a mile or two to that."

"Okay, so that makes about fourteen miles." Wes scratched his head. "And, Dad, you've told us that most people hike about two miles per hour. So, it should take them about seven hours to get here."

Amber was already doing the math in her head. "That means they should arrive back here at around *one a.m.*"

Wes looked at the clock on the dash. It was only 10:15.

He sighed and fell back into his seat between Amber and Jake.

"Get comfortable, guys." Uncle Brian stretched and yawned. "This is going to be a long night."

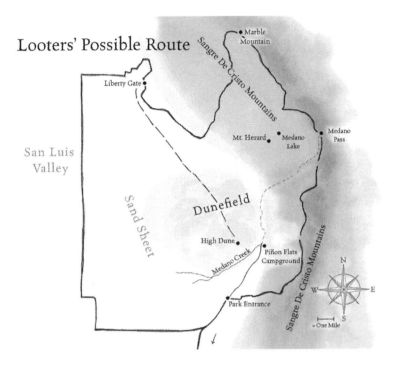

CHAPTER 7

1880 - HATCHET GASH

Emma and Gideon continued their descent through the forest until they found the creek. There the ground became more steep and rocky. Above them, the mountainsides formed a tight V-shape, narrowing to the creek bed. At their feet, the ground fell away into a deep gorge. This was Hatchet Gash, and from here, it looked like the only way through the chasm was to plunge over the edge. But some time ago, she had found a way through. With the wild green growth of summer, things had changed. Emma's eyes searched for the spot, and her heart clenched at the thought of missing it.

She guided Gideon by his reins, gently pulling left to the south side of the gash. They walked alongside the coarse, gray surface of an enormous boulder. More towers of rock, many the size of cabins, lined the rim of the gash like a wall created by giants in some ancient time beyond memory. Aspen trees filled the spaces in between. Their leaves fluttered in the cool winds that were channeled from the mountaintops into this hidden canyon. She rubbed and patted the horse's neck. "We'll find it, Gideon. We've done it before, and I know you can do it again."

They stepped slowly now. Emma scanned her memory as she stared into the gaps between the rocks, hoping to spot the passage. Then it appeared: an aspen tree had split into three trunks at its base. Emma let out a sigh of relief. Behind the tree was just enough space for the horse to slide between its third trunk and the face of the enormous boulder. Gideon saw the spot, and let out a nervous snort, quiet and low.

Emma got down from the saddle and tried to soothe her panicked horse. "I don't want to do this either, but it's the only way we can escape."

At the word "escape," Gideon's eyes went from worried to wild as a long howl echoed along the canyon walls.

Emma pressed her forehead against his. "You and I have been through it all. And we'll get through this, too. I promise. I just need you to trust me."

Behind the twisted aspen trunks, two boulders overlapped one another, concealing a narrow pathway between the rocks. Gideon could squeeze through only if he was unburdened, so Emma unfastened his saddlebag and threw it over her shoulder. She untied the dog and carried him in her arms, grasping Gideon's reigns with her right hand to lead him into the gap.

They slid through the slot and into the tight passage between the rocks. As they walked, the granite walls pressed against Gideon's flanks. He breathed through his nose, making Emma aware of just how nervous her horse was in such a confined space. She knew that all of Gideon's senses were telling him that he was trapped and that their pursuers were near. She also knew the hounds might try to follow them, but she was sure the other horses would refuse. No horse was as brave as Gideon. And even if the men somehow made it to the other side of the passage, they wouldn't have the nerve to follow them down into Hatchet Gash.

CHAPTER 8

EMPTY-HANDED

Waiting for hours in Ranger Trujillo's truck made it clear to the kids that being a ranger wasn't always full of excitement. Staring out the window at dark nothing, hoping to see the beam of a flashlight, was about the most boring activity Jake could imagine. To pass the time, they started telling stories and playing a dice game Wes had brought with him. Ranger Trujillo told them about two ghost towns that were a short hike from where they were parked. The dilapidated barns and cabins were now overtaken by prairie grass and sagebrush. To Jake, it felt kind of creepy to think of those buildings standing alone and deserted in the darkness.

Midnight passed with no sign of the three looters. After another hour of waiting, Wes began to nod off. Then, just past 2 a.m., Jake nudged his cousin awake.

"That was weird," Wes mumbled. "I dreamed I was a buffalo wandering around in the desert looking for water."

"Look!" Jake pointed through the windshield at two small white lights bobbing up and down in the distance.

"It's the headlamps of two hikers," Uncle Brian said. "Wes, your time estimate was pretty close."

"But there are only two of them," Wes said.

"Maybe," Ranger Trujillo replied. "It could be that one of them doesn't have a light and is following the others." His face turned serious as he locked eyes with each of the kids. "When they get here, I'm going to turn on the truck's headlights. We'll keep the cab dark so they can't see you. I want you three to study them and see if they are the same people you saw at the pond."

"Sure thing," Jake said. Amber and Wes nodded in agreement. As the lights grew closer to the trailhead, tension built inside Jake's chest. He could hear his heart beating. When the hikers reached the lot, Ranger Trujillo flipped on the lights and stepped out. Jake saw the sheriff slide out of his vehicle to join them. Ranger Trujillo's greeting was audible through the open windows.

"Good evening, folks," he called out in a friendly voice.

Jake could see the two hikers talking, but he couldn't make out their words over the purr of the truck's diesel engine. Ranger Trujillo led the gray figures into the rays of the headlights. Immediately, Jake recognized them.

"That's them," Amber whispered. "The girl with the ball cap and the guy with the cargo pants. But where's the other guy with the ponytail?"

"Yeah, that's for sure the people we saw." Wes put his hand on his dad's shoulder. "Look, guys, he's going to check their packs."

The young woman and man took off their tan camo backpacks and sat them at Ranger Trujillo's feet. He opened them and looked inside.

"Please wait here for a moment," he said to the hikers. He walked to the truck window and looked at the kids. "Do you guys recognize them?"

"Yes," Jake replied. "Those are the people we saw. But the guy with the long hair isn't with them."

"Thanks. I'll be back in a few minutes."

He stepped back into the beams of the headlights, pulled out a pad of paper, and took a few notes. The backpackers slung their packs over their shoulders, walked over to their white SUV, opened its back hatch, and set their gear inside.

While Ranger Trujillo talked with the sheriff, the hikers backed up their vehicle and pulled out of the parking lot. From his side window, Jake watched its red taillights fade into the distance.

A few moments later, the truck door opened, and

Ranger Trujillo got back into the cab. "Well, kids, it looks like we've got a mystery on our hands."

"Why'd you just let them go?" Wes asked.

"I can't detain them unless there's evidence they took something."

"But they did," Wes replied. "We saw them."

"I believe you. But I searched their bags, and they only had gear in there. No artifacts."

"What about the third guy?" Jake asked.

"That's where things get even more interesting. I asked them if they were expecting anyone else from their party. They said it was just the two of them."

"They totally lied to you." Wes shook his head in exasperation.

"I took down their names and phone numbers, and the sheriff ran their license plate. So, we've got the information we need to call them in for questioning when we get some proof. And I expect that's going to happen." Ranger Trujillo put the truck in reverse, turned it around, and began the long drive back to the campground.

Wes slumped back into his seat and sighed. "I feel like we stayed up all night for nothing."

"Don't let it get you down," Ranger Trujillo said. "These things take patience. Without you three, I wouldn't have been able to get a positive identification of those two. And the Parks Service has already dispatched an agent from the ISB. She'll be here in the morning."

"The ISB?" Amber asked.

"It's the Investigative Services Branch of the National Parks Service."

"So, the agent, she's a detective?" Jake asked.

"Sure is. They investigate crimes like looting, poaching, and other unsavory stuff that might occur within the boundaries of the National Parks."

"Does she carry a gun, like you?" Wes asked. "I mean, I've noticed that some rangers do, and others don't."

"You're observant, Wes. Some of us are Law Enforcement Rangers, and our job is to keep folks accountable to the laws that govern the national parks. We're a lot like police officers. And yes, Agent Colter is also considered an enforcement ranger, so she carries a sidearm, like me."

"Cool." Wes yawned and fought to keep his eyes open.

"Jake," Amber whispered, "you should ask him about Caverna Del Oro and Elmyra Holcomb."

Jake started to speak but hesitated. He whispered to Amber, "I don't know. It feels too risky."

"He grew up here. He'll know." Amber whispered back. "We've only got *two more days* before we have to leave. You need to ask him now."

"What are you kids whispering about?" Uncle Brian asked.

"Jake has a question for Ranger Trujillo." Amber looked at Jake, her mischievous smile only visible to him in the near darkness.

He glared at her, then cleared his throat. "Mr. Trujillo, do you know anything about the Caverna Del Oro?"

Ranger Trujillo laughed. "Well, you picked a perfect story to tell at two in the morning."

Wes's eyes popped open as if his sleepiness had melted into the night, and he leaned forward again. "Is it real then?

"Kind of," Trujillo explained. "It's a real place, way up there in the mountains. But the legends surrounding it are probably just myths. According to the story, way back in the 1400s, a group of Spanish conquistadors arrived in the San Luis Valley. They made their way into the mountains and came upon a cave entrance on the side of Marble Mountain. When they went to explore the cavern, they discovered gold. One version of the story says they loaded up all the gold and made their way back to Mexico. But other versions say they built a set of thick wooden doors to one of the chambers, hid the gold inside, and locked it away."

"Has anyone been down in there since?" Amber asked.

"Oh, yeah. In the 1800s, a local pioneer, Elisha Horn, was climbing Marble Mountain and reported finding a skeleton still covered in Spanish armor with an arrow through the back. Nearby, he found a red Maltese cross painted on the rock. Beside the cross, he discovered the entrance to the cavern. Later, explorers found stuff down in there, like ropes and a bucket, a mining hammer, and a wooden ladder. But no gold."

"How do you get there?" Jake asked.

"Oh, it's a long ways from the dunes, probably twenty miles from Piñon Flats. And you'd have to go with professional rock climbers and cavers. I've been through the first forty feet or so of the entrance, but after that, it's a sheer drop-off—one-hundred-and-fifty feet straight down into darkness."

Jake's shoulders slumped. He was exhausted and now disheartened. *Twenty miles away and one hundred and fifty feet straight down? That would be impossible to get to! What was grandpa thinking? Would he really make this so difficult and dangerous?*

"The name," Amber whispered. "Ask him about the Holcomb lady."

"I will," Jake whispered back. His words came out tired and curt. "Just be patient, okay." As soon as he responded, he wished he had not been so short with her. He squared his shoulders. "Thanks for telling us the story, Mr. Trujillo. I was also wondering, do you know anything about somebody named...Elmyra Holcomb."

"Now that's a name I wasn't expecting," Trujillo said. "How in the world do you know about Miss Elmyra?"

Jake wasn't exactly sure how to respond, so he just told the truth. "I think my grandfather must have known her."

"Well, it just so happens that I was planning on paying her a visit to tell her about your little discovery. Miss Elmyra is considered one of the historians of the San Luis Valley. When I've got questions about the past, she's the one I ask. In fact, she's the last person around here who can remember seeing one of the interdunal ponds. Would you kids like to meet her?"

"Definitely," Jake replied.

"When do you all leave?" Ranger Trujillo asked.

"We're here for a couple more days and leave on Wednesday morning," Jake replied.

"I could take you three over to meet her on Tuesday."

Wes leaned forward. "Dad, do you think we could?"

Uncle Brian stifled a yawn. "I'll need to run it by the other parents. We have a picnic planned up near Zapata Falls that day, but I bet we can make your meeting happen."

"For now, let's plan to head over to the Holcomb place sometime in the morning before your picnic," Ranger Trujillo said. "You guys are going to love Zapata Falls. It's really unusual. It's almost like a waterfall inside a cave."

For the rest of the drive home, Uncle Brian and

Ranger Trujillo continued talking about farming and water and what it was like to grow up in such a remote part of Colorado. But the kids didn't hear them because they had all three fallen asleep. They didn't awaken until four o'clock in the morning when the truck pulled into Piñon Flats. Ranger Trujillo thanked them for their help, and they all trudged across the asphalt into their campers, where they collapsed in their beds and feel back to sleep.

CHAPTER 9

1880 - THE PASSAGE

Emma peered down into the bottom of Hatch Gash to where Cold Creek ran like a thin ribbon of silver through the bottom of the canyon. The dog whined as she gently set him down on Gideon's back and again secured him with the leather straps. She could see where one of his wounds was still seeping blood and soaking into his yellow fur. "It's going to be rough, boy. But we're going to make it." She turned, gripped Gideon's bridle in her right hand, and began choosing her steps down the side of the canyon.

The hounds were at the gap now. They howled and bayed, their way of telling the men that they had picked up the retriever's scent. When the men finally squeezed their way through the passage, Emma and Gideon were out of sight. The men stared down into the canyon. Though they feared returning to their boss empty-handed, they wouldn't risk such a perilous path.

"I say we give the dogs a rest, Carver," the shorter man said. "Then we make our way down through the woods. If that stupid animal is going that way—" he pointed down into Hatchet Gash— "then we'll likely find him in a pile at the bottom."

Carver agreed, and they paused their hunt to let their dogs and horses rest.

It had been an hour since she had last heard the barks and howls. Emma would have been relieved if she were not constantly concerned that her dear horse, at any moment, might slip and plunge down the canyon wall. Step by step, they made their way over wobbly rocks and slick gravel. Eventually, they arrived at the overhang. In front of them, a slim path of loose soil and pebbles ran along the foot of a slanted rock wall. Gideon would have to keep his hooves against the wall and bow his neck low to press through. Emma could see his muscles tense. But if she could lead Gideon across the next ten yards, they would be out of this mess.

"You've got this, Gideon. Come on." She coaxed him forward onto the impossible path.

Step after agonizing step, she guided the horse through until the overhang gave way to a wide path of coarse gravel on the other side.

"You did it, boy!" She hugged his neck. "I knew you would."

Gideon exhaled a proud snort.

They worked their way down to Cold Creek at the bottom of the canyon, then followed its course until the trees and undergrowth gave way to a landscape of swirling sand. The Great Sand Dunes stretched from Emma's feet into the sky. At the sight, she let out a long sigh of relief.

With level ground under his hooves, Gideon could move faster now, but he was growing weary. He drank from the creek and grazed on the green grass that grew along its banks while Emma checked on the dog. He had gone completely limp. She put her cheek to his dry nose and could feel his faint, warm breath on her skin. He was still alive, but she was losing him. They had to get home fast.

CHAPTER 10

THE SAND RAMP TRAIL

Jake smelled pancakes—or maybe it was waffles. Whatever it was, it smelled good enough to wake him up. He rubbed the sleep out of his eyes, put on his hiking pants and a T-shirt, then stepped out of the empty camper in his bare feet. Amber was already up and sitting at the picnic table. Her dad was cooking breakfast at the fold-down kitchen attached to the side of their camper.

"Good morning, Jake," Mr. Catalina said. "Want some sausage and pancakes?"

"Yes, thank you," he answered. "I'm so hungry."

"Well, it's about 10 a.m.; I'm sure well past your usual breakfast time."

Jake looked around, noticing how quiet and empty the campsite felt. "Where is everyone?"

"Wes is still sleeping," Amber replied. "And the rest of the parents went to hike the Montville Trail. They should be back soon."

"Thanks for staying to make us breakfast, Mr. Catalina," Jake said.

"My pleasure." He plopped three big pancakes onto a plate and handed it to Jake. "You three had quite a night helping track down the looters."

A loud crash came from inside Wes's RV, followed by the clatter of several more items falling and hitting the floor. The door opened, and Wes walked out still in his pajamas with a blanket wrapped around him. He didn't say a word but trudged over to the picnic table and sat down between Jake and Amber.

"Good morning, Wes," Mr. Catalina said.

Wes answered with a grunt. He wasn't being rude. He just wasn't able to form words yet. Mr. Catalina smiled and set a plate full of steaming, buttermilk pancakes in front of him. "Maybe this will revive you."

Mr. Catalina set out a jug of maple syrup, then placed three mugs on the table and began filling them with coffee.

"Coffee?" Jake gave him a puzzled look.

"This might be the day you start drinking it," Mr. Catalina said. "I've never seen three more sleepy-looking people in all my life."

Jake took a sip and turned his face up at the bitter

taste. "Is there maybe something I could put in it to make it taste better?"

Mr. Catalina returned with some vanilla sweet cream, and all three kids poured so much of it into their mugs that their drinks became more like coffee-flavored milkshakes.

"That's more like it," Wes said.

"He speaks!" Mr. Catalina joked. "I knew the coffee would do the trick."

With breakfast served, Amber's dad grabbed a book from inside their camper and sat in a chair to read on the other side of the campfire ring. He was far enough away that he would not be able to hear their conversation, and Jake wondered if he'd done that on purpose, to give the kids some privacy.

"I think I know where they hid the stuff," Wes whispered.

"You think they stashed the artifacts somewhere?" Amber asked.

"I do. That guy with the long hair. He couldn't have carried it all by himself," Wes explained. "And between the Dunes and the Liberty Gate, there's just a bunch of sand and grass. So they would've stashed it somewhere closer to the mountains where there are more trees and rocks to hide the bags."

Jake went into the camper and came back with his map

of Great Sand Dunes National Park. He took another bite of his pancakes, moved his plate aside, and unfolded the map on the table.

"So, if we saw them here just below High Dune—" Jake pointed to the X that marked High Dune— "and they went to the Liberty Gate, that would have taken them across this big prairie." He traced the route along the map with his finger, and then looked up at his cousin. "But, Wes—if you're right—they would have first hiked straight North, to where the dunefield ends right here at the base of the mountains." His finger landed on the dashed line of a trail.

Wes nodded as he finished chewing. "Remember how I said the looters should have arrived at one in the morning? But they got to the Liberty Gate after *two*. They were an hour late because they took a longer route and spent time hiding the stuff."

"But why?" Amber asked.

Wes shrugged. "I don't know. Maybe they knew it was too risky to hike out with it. But I know where I would have hidden it." He put his finger on the map where a blue stream crossed the trail. "There's a gulch right here where this creek crosses the Sand Ramp Trail. That would be the perfect place."

Jake took out a pen, found the Sand Ramp Trail, and began marking out the miles on the map. "That's like *seven* miles from here. There's no way we could get there today."

"We could if the hike was shorter," Wes offered. "My Dad could drive us in his jeep up this four-wheel-drive road and drop us off at the trail. That would make it a three-and-a-half-mile hike to the creek."

"We'd have to go as soon as our parents got back." Jake

tapped his finger on the map. "If we want to convince them quickly, we're going to need an itinerary."

The previous week, while they were still in Rocky Mountain National Park, their parents had made a deal with them. Jake, Amber, and Wes could venture out on hikes together, without their parents, if they did several things. First, they had to plan out an itinerary that listed the trails they would take, pack appropriate supplies, and set their estimated time of arrival (their ETA). They also had to carry the emergency beacon. Finally, they absolutely had to arrive back on time.

Jake looked over the map and figured the hike would take them about four to five hours. When the parents returned to the campground, the three kids sat down with Uncle Brian to review their plans. Uncle Brian had led survival training exercises in the army, so the adults trusted him to review their plans and make sure the kids were prepared.

"Have you three checked the weather?" Uncle Brian asked.

"We have," Jake answered. "It's going to be a clear day."

"What do you think your greatest risk will be then?"

"The sun," Wes replied. "That's why we've packed a lot of extra water."

"Good thinking," Uncle Brian said. "And make sure you all are wearing hats and sunscreen."

"Got it." Jake patted the side of his backpack.

"Did you pack the emergency beacon?"

"Right here." Wes patted his backpack.

"Sounds like you three are ready." Uncle Brian spun his keyring around on his finger. "Let's load up."

They climbed into the jeep and began their drive up Medano Pass Road. Uncle Brian had removed the doors and the soft top. Amber's hair blew in the wind as they made their way up the mountainside. When they passed a sign that read *Point of No Return*, Wes turned to Jake. "Well, that's not very encouraging."

The jeep bumped and crawled along the rock-strewn road. As it climbed, they could now look down on the sand dunes.

"Wow, you can see the whole dunefield from up here," Amber said. "And I bet the Liberty Gate is way up that way." She pointed to the north. "No wonder it took us so long to get there last night."

The short piñon pines that filled their campground and lined the Medano Pass Road now gave way to taller ponderosa pine trees. Uncle Brian pulled the jeep over, stopped, and got out. "Follow me, guys."

"But Dad, we've got a schedule," Wes moaned.

"This will only take a few minutes."

"Where are we going?"

"You'll see."

They followed a faint path until it merged with a wider one into a grove of big, old trees. Uncle Brian knelt down to inspect one of them.

"Come here and check this out." He patted the ground near the tree. "See how the bark is pulled away from the base of the tree?"

"Yeah. Is it from a lightning strike?" Amber asked.

"Good guess," Uncle Brian replied. "But if that were the case, we would likely see burn marks, too."

"I bet someone tried to chop the thing down and got too tired to finish," Wes guessed.

Ponderosa Pine
Bark Peels

"You're right that it was the work of people, but they

weren't trying to kill the tree. Over two hundred years ago, the Ute people would peel segments of bark off these ponderosa pines. They'd use the bark to make baskets and medicines and the sap and pitch as glue."

"Looks like they knew how to do it without killing the trees." Jake ran his fingers over the scars, then looked up into the treetops. "These things are huge."

"Dad, this is cool and all, but we're kinda hoping to get on the trail," Wes said.

His dad stood up and dusted off the dirt from his knees. "All right, let's get going."

They hurried back to the jeep, got in, and continued up the Medano Pass Road. The jeep crawled along, kicking up a cloud of dust behind it. After another mile, Uncle Brian spotted a sign for the Sand Creek Trailhead and steered the jeep into a pullout.

"Looks like we're here." Uncle Brian glanced down at his watch. "I'll see you guys back here at five p.m."

"Thanks, Dad."

Wes jumped out of the jeep, followed by Jake and Amber. Uncle Brian put the jeep in gear and continued up the road. It soon disappeared around a bend, and the thrum of its engine faded until the only sound left was the wind blowing through the trees.

"This way, guys!" Wes jogged across the road and onto a sand-filled trail. "Let's go find some stolen treasure."

CHAPTER 11

1880 - HOME

"Darling, where have you been?" The old rancher asked as he met Emma and Gideon coming into the ranch. "And what is that you've got draped over your horse?"

"It's a dog." She dismounted and started untying the leather straps.

"We were beginning to get worried about ya," Mr. Herard said, his French accent flavoring his words. Mr. Herard had gentle eyes and a soft, gray and white mustache. Suspenders held up his denim jeans, and he wore a weathered, thick-brimmed hat that his wife could not convince him to replace. When she tried, he would say, "It's serving me just fine." Mrs. Herard found Ulysses Herard completely incorrigible. But Emma always thought of him as kind.

He helped her carry the dog into the barn, where he prepared a bed of fresh straw. "I'll fetch him some jerky from the smokehouse. Emma, how 'bout you get him something to drink."

She drew water from the creek and cleaned the dog's wounds while Mr. Herard fed the retriever several thin strips of beef.

"So, you found 'im up on the mountain?" he asked.

"In the woods near Medano Lake. There were men and hounds tracking him like he was a mountain lion."

"Now that's curious." Mr. Herard adjusted the hat. "Well, he's safe now. And I guess he's yours now, too."

After caring for the dog, Emma brushed Gideon, got him some fresh water and hay, and joined the Herard family for dinner. The sun had set, and they ate by the light of kerosene lanterns. Mr. Herard had just raised his fork to his mouth when a pounding came at the cabin door. He pushed his chair back from the table, took his rifle down from the wall, and walked to the door. Sliding aside the wooden latch, he cracked it open.

"What's your business, fellas?"

Emma could hear a man's voice. "We're sorry to disturb you, sir. We got a bit turned around on the mountain today and are running low on food."

"I'll see what I can do." Mr. Herard stepped out into

the night and closed the door behind him. About twenty minutes later, he returned, hung his rifle back on the wall, and sat down to his cold dinner.

"That was awful nice of you, Ulysses," Mrs. Herard said.

Mr. Herard nodded and took a bite of his food. "There were two of 'em. Said they had lost a dog and had been tracking him."

Emma's heart stopped beating. Mr. Herard looked at her, and, from the glint in his eyes, she knew he understood how worried she was. "Don't fret, child. The dog is safe in the barn."

He continued eating. A moment later, he tapped a finger on the table. "You can tell an honest man by the way he talks, by the way he looks ya in the eyes...or avoids ya. Them two were shifty."

The next morning Emma woke, washed her face, and got dressed for the day. As she walked out to the barn, the sun was rising over the mountains and lighting up the valley below. She opened the barn door, and in the soft, orange light, she could see Gideon in his stall. She looked to the bed of straw Mr. Herard had made for the dog. He was gone.

CHAPTER 12

THE DROP

"I thought this was supposed to be a trail." Wes shook his head and looped his fingers under the straps of his backpack. "There's more sand than dirt or rocks on this trail. It feels more like hiking up one of the dunes."

"This is definitely not what I expected." Amber craned her neck to see further up the path. "But maybe things will change."

"I sure hope so because all this sand is slowing us down," Jake grumbled. "If the trail stays like this, then there's no way we're going to get back on time." He could already feel the sand that had worked its way inside of his boots.

The trail arched uphill. The vast dunefield was on their left, and the mountains rose into the sky on their right. From this vantage point, they could see what Ranger

Trujillo had explained last night, how the winds from the west were pushing and piling the sand into the green foothills. Grain by grain, the yellow blanket crept up the lower slopes of the Sangre De Cristo Mountains.

Soon they saw trees up ahead, but as they got closer, it proved only to be a thin strip of woods growing along a narrow creek. Amber jumped back as something darted past her and ran up the trunk of a nearby tree.

"Did you guys see that thing?" she exclaimed.

Jake froze in his tracks, thinking perhaps she had seen a bear. "No, what was it?"

"I don't know." Amber took a few cautious steps toward the tree. "It was like a squirrel, but it was *huge* and black."

"I think I see it." Jake followed her and crept toward the tree, trying not to scare the creature away.

Wes stayed put, letting the others investigate.

Just above their heads, a pointed black face peered out from behind the tree trunk. It looked like a squirrel, but it was at least three times as big as any squirrel Jake had ever seen. Tufts of black and gray hair curled off the tips of its long ears.

Wes cautiously joined his cousin and Amber to get a better look at the animal. "Do you think we've discovered some kind of new species?"

"Don't be silly, Wes," Amber said. "I've heard about these things. But I forget what they're called. They live up here in the mountains. We should look them up in your guidebook when we get back."

The black squirrel crept out further onto the branch, where they could now see his long bushy tail. Amber took several pictures of it before they continued hiking.

The trail descended through the trees, crossed the creek, then climbed again into a swirling low plain of dunes. Prairie grass and sagebrush began to overtake the sand. The sage left a sweet, cool scent in the air as they passed through it.

"Hey guys, I've got another riddle for you," Wes said.

Jake sighed, and Amber shook her head.

"What do you call a bear without an ear?"

Jake thought about it for a moment before giving up. "I really don't know."

"It's a B," Wes said, very much pleased with himself.

"I don't get it," Jake replied.

Wes grimaced. "You know. Bear is spelled with a *B*, then an 'ear.' If you take off the e-a-r, all you have left is the *B*."

Amber shook her head and laughed under her breath. "That's just goofy."

"Okay, see if you can figure this next one out," Wes said. "What color socks do bears wear?"

"I'd say brown," Amber replied. "But it depends on what kind of bear. Like a black bear, of course, would wear black socks, and a polar bear would probably wear white socks."

"That's a good guess." Wes grinned. "But they actually don't wear socks because they have *bear* feet."

"Oh, that's so terrible." Jake rolled his eyes and looked to the sky, partly because he should have known the answer, and because the answer was so ridiculous.

"Wes, where in the world do you get these things?" Amber asked.

"From my dad."

"That figures; they remind me of dad jokes," Amber replied.

They were grateful to see aspen trees up ahead, dotting the landscape along the trail. Any shade was a welcome relief from the unrelenting sun.

"We should stop there to have a drink up there." Jake pointed ahead. "We don't want to get dehydrated."

They found a spot in the shade of one of the bigger trees and drank from their water bottles. The aspen's leaves rustled in the wind and cast flittering shadows across the ground. Wes opened his backpack and pulled out the map.

"We might be getting close. I think this area is the Aspen Campground, and that—" Wes pointed to the east — "is called Heavenly Valley."

Jake turned to where Wes pointed to see a broad, green meadow surrounded by clusters of aspen trees. Above the valley loomed the enormous snow-capped peak of Mount Herard. "It's getting hot, and I don't want to leave this shade." He took off his hat and wiped the sweat from his brow. He could feel the grit of dust and sand on his lips. "But we should keep moving."

They packed up their water bottles and continued hiking north up the trail. Jake noticed that Wes, who was usually talkative, had grown quiet.

"Can you believe that just a few days ago, we were in snow deep enough to swallow, Jake?" Amber mused. "And today we're in a *desert*?"

"Wait till we get to the Grand Canyon," Jake said. "That's going to be wild. I hear it can get super cold, with snow up at the top, and be over a hundred degrees down at the bottom."

Wes remained silent, hiking ahead of the line.

"Is he okay?" Amber whispered. "It's not like him to be so quiet."

"I know. I was thinking the same thing." Jake whispered back.

Wes, who had been hiking at a fast pace, slowed and stood still. He turned to face Jake and Amber.

"What's up, Wes?" Jake asked.

"Yeah, are you okay?" Amber's eyes narrowed in concern.

Wes nodded. "I guess I'm just afraid that I'll be wrong about this. That the looters didn't hide the bags out here."

"If you are," Jake said, "it won't be a big deal."

"It feels like a big deal." Wes hung his head and nudged a rock with his boot. "I mean, back at school, no one listens to me. Nobody takes me seriously. But you guys are different. You believed in my idea right away, and you *followed* me out here into the middle of nowhere."

"You're right, Wes," Amber said. "We did. Because we think you're smart. And we trust you."

"Yeah...but what if I'm wrong?"

"It won't matter to us." She took a step closer to Wes. "We believed you and followed the plan because we all thought your idea was a good one."

He nudged the rock with his boot again, then raised his eyes to look at Amber and Jake. "Thanks, guys."

Jake gave his cousin a playful punch on the shoulder. "Remember what you guys told me at Emerald Lake? You said, 'We're *a team*.' And right now, *our team* has made a decision to follow *you*."

Wes pulled his hands from his pockets and adjusted his pack. "Then let's do this thing." He turned around and continued up the trail.

They soon crested the brow of the hill they had been climbing. From the bluff, they looked down upon a strip of green that cut its way through the wind-bent and brown grasses of the sand field.

"That's where I think they went." Wes pointed below and to his right. "Down there to where the creek flows out of the mountains."

Jake couldn't see any water. "There's a creek down there?"

"Yeah, that's why it's all green," Wes replied. "I bet they followed it up into that gulch."

The kids jogged down the hillside as fast as they could to the creekbed. Amber stopped and knelt close to the ground. "Guys, come look at this!"

The boys ran to her side.

"See these boot prints?" She traced one of the tracks with her finger. "They came from that way." She stood up and pointed toward the dunes. "And they head this way." She turned around and pointed upstream. "Wes, you were right."

They quickened their pace, following the prints until the sandy ground became dirt and rock. Trees and green undergrowth choked their path.

"Do you guys see any more footprints?" Jake asked.

They all stopped to look around.

"Over here," Amber called out. "There's some in the mud where they crossed the creek."

Following the boot prints, they eventually came to a

jagged wall of gray rock that cut through the gulch. To Jake, it looked like the backbone and fins of some half-buried prehistoric animal. The sawtooth wall of rock abruptly ended in the creek, where the quiet waters flowed around its dark and lichen-covered surface. He immediately latched onto the fin of rock and inched his way around the obstacle.

He hadn't expected to see this on the other side. The wall of rock curved up the slope of the gulch and arched overhead, casting its shadow across the ground and onto the ends of his boots. Stepping into the shadow, he paused until his eyes adjusted, and he could make out a wide recess in the rock, like a shallow cave.

"You guys have got to see this!" he called out.

Amber and Wes followed his example and scrambled their way around the rock wall.

"Over here!" Jake yelled from the dark alcove. "It's like a cave, but it doesn't go back very far."

Wes dug out his headlamp and turned it on. They could now see another low wall of rock. When they got to the other side of it, the light caught the sheen of something glossy and blue.

"You're kidding me!" Wes pressed into the gap alongside Jake. It was a blue nylon dry bag—the exact same kind the looters had used.

"Why are you so surprised?" Jake elbowed his cousin. "I mean, you're the one who guessed it."

"But I was *guessing*. I wasn't certain about it."

"Well, now you can be certain," Amber said. She stepped into the light and snapped open the thick plastic buckle that held the bag closed. Inside, on top, she found a piece of folded paper and handed it to Jake. The light of Wes' headlamp revealed several large pieces of pottery bundled in clear plastic bubble wrap. These were definitely some of the artifacts from the pond.

They heard voices.

Jake's eyes grew wide in the dull light. "We've got to hide, and quick." He stuffed the paper into his back pocket.

"Let's take the bag." Wes tugged on it, but it was too heavy.

"We've got to go, and *now*," Jake warned. "Leave it."

Amber fastened the buckle, and they sprinted out of the alcove. Scrambling up the hillside, they found a place to hide behind a boulder. Just as they made it out of sight, two men climbed around the barrier, making their way into the alcove the same way the kids had entered. One of the men carried a GPS unit.

The men's clothing looked out of place. Instead of hiking gear, they wore dark pants and dress shirts, now soaked with sweat. Sunglasses covered their eyes.

"This marks the spot of the drop," one man said, his voice calm and determined.

"Must be in here," the other replied, disappearing into the darkness of the alcove. The first man followed. There was a long pause.

Finally, the calm voice echoed from the alcove: "I thought he said there would be *more*."

"This must be all they found," replied the other. "But the Director will be happy. This might be exactly what he's been looking for."

Just as quickly as the men had appeared, they climbed back around the rock wall, one of them with the blue pack flung over his shoulder.

Jake looked at Amber and Wes, putting his forefinger

to his lips so they would stay silent. Wes looked like he was going to explode if he didn't talk. After a couple of minutes, Jake nodded to signal that he thought it was safe.

"Those were the *same* guys who were after us at Twin Owls," Wes whispered. "When we were in Rocky Mountain National Park."

"It was *definitely* them." Amber shook her head in disbelief.

"That's what we should call them." Wes's eyes lit up like he had discovered something. "It's perfect because there are *two* of them." He held up two fingers, then let them fall to his side.

Jake squished his eyebrows together. "Call them what?"

"The *Twin Owls*."

"That's clever," Amber said. "It's like we've got our own codename for the bad guys."

Jake stood up and stared at the alcove. "They said they were working for some guy they called *The Director*. That must be who hired the looters and had them hide the artifacts here."

"What's on that paper?" Amber gestured to the now crumpled sheet jammed into Jake's back pocket.

He unfolded it and read it out loud: "This bag is one of three. I want ten times your original price. 13000604 Fatal Plazas."

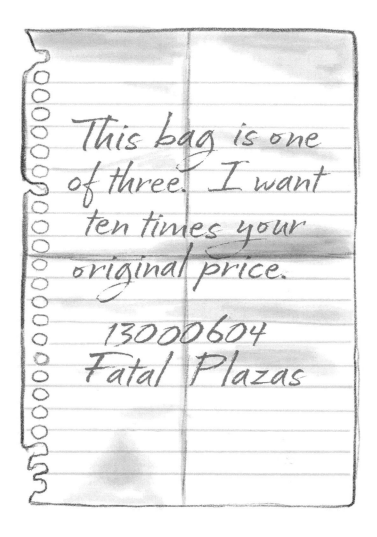

This bag is one of three. I want ten times your original price.

13000604
Fatal Plazas

CHAPTER 13

1880 - FIX'N TO RUN

Emma drew in a deep breath, trying to calm her heart and mind. The men must have found him and taken him in the night. She imagined them sneaking into the barn and finding him on the bed of straw. Then she noticed a thin length of rope secured to one of the barn beams. It stretched taut from the beam to the back corner of the barn. She followed the rope into the corner where the dirt floor met the wood siding of the wall. The dirt had been dug away, creating a gap just big enough for a dog to slip through. Then the rope moved. Emma turned and ran out the door and around the barn to find the dog lunging and trying to break free from his makeshift leash.

She approached the yellow dog as he struggled against the tight line that was now holding him close to the side of the barn. Holding out her hands, she spoke softly to him, "Hey, boy. Let me help you." He turned, looked into her eyes, and his raspy, labored breathing slowed. She stepped closer and pulled the dog toward her to take the tension off of the rope.

From behind her came the sound of Mr. Herard's voice. "I checked on him before turnin' in last night, and I could tell he was fix'n to run." He knelt beside them and began untying the rope from the dog's leather collar.

"What should we do?" Emma held the scruff of the dog's neck so that he couldn't bolt into the forest.

"I think we've got to let him go," Mr. Herard answered.

"But those men—they might find him. And who knows what else he might run into on the mountain?"

Mr. Herard thought for a moment. "How about you saddle up our horses, Emma."

"Why?"

"Because we're going to follow him."

CHAPTER 14

THE BEACON

"We've got to get back and tell someone before the Twin Owls get away," Jake said. "Amber, can you get a signal?"

She had scrambled up the hillside to check for cell reception. Holding the phone out in front of her as she walked, she made her way back to the boys. "Nothing." Amber slipped the phone back into her pocket, slid a hair tie off of her wrist, and pulled her hair back into a ponytail. Jake could tell she was preparing to run back to the trailhead.

"What if we use the beacon?" Wes asked. "Remember, it doesn't need a cell signal."

"I don't know," Jake said. "If we hit the button, then our parents will think one of us got hurt or lost, and they'll send out a search-and-rescue team to find us."

"Exactly!" Amber replied. "The Twin Owls must have parked at the Liberty Gate or back where Wes's dad dropped us off. So, if we hit the button on the beacon, then there's a good chance the search-and-rescue people might see the Twin Owls along the trail—and maybe even stop them."

"You're right." Jake agreed, but his voice was still hesitant. "The thing is, if we press the beacon, search-and-rescue won't be looking for the Twin Owls." He shook his head. "They'll be looking for *us*. I'm just afraid—" he stopped mid-sentence.

"Afraid of what?" Amber asked.

"I'm...afraid that if we freak our parents out, they're not going to let us hike on our own anymore."

All three kids were quiet for a few moments. Then Wes punched his fist into the palm of his other hand. "I think we should do it. You're right. It will probably freak our parents out, but they'll understand when they hear what happened. Plus, search-and-rescue will have radios, which means we'll have a way to contact the rangers."

He pulled the orange device out of his pack and held his thumb over the button. "Are we all okay with this?" He looked to Jake, then to Amber.

"No," Jake shouted.

At the same time, Amber said, "Yes."

Jake reached for the beacon—but he wasn't fast enough.

Wes pressed the button. A tiny green light on the front began flashing.

Wes stared at the green blinking light as though he was waiting for the device to do something more. "Well, that was a letdown." He gave the beacon a shake.

"What did you think was going to happen?" Amber asked.

"I don't know." Wes shrugged. "Maybe at least it would beep or vibrate or something. You know, like those things they give you at restaurants that tell you when your table is ready."

Jake clenched his jaw and turned to walk away. Spinning around, he glared at Wes. "Why did you do that?" His voice tinged with the anger he was trying to hold back. "We didn't agree."

"It was two to one, Jake."

"Guys, we don't have time to argue," Amber said. "We pressed it. Now we've got to get moving."

"*We* didn't press it. *Wes* pressed it. And now you guys just put the whole scavenger hunt at risk!" Jake raised his hands in frustration and began walking toward the creek. But no footsteps followed him. Turning back, he saw Wes and Amber standing stock still. He could tell they were taken aback by his reaction.

"Are you guys coming, or what?" He asked. It was a question, but it came out more like a demand. "The faster we get back, the faster we can tell the rangers about the Twin Owls."

In an uncomfortable silence, they joined Jake and crept back around the rock wall. Jake stewed. *I'll have to explain to the search and rescue people how we weren't really lost. And why we decided to press the beacon.* He imagined his mom; how worried she must be, wondering if one of them was hurt. But the worst part would be facing Uncle Brian and admitting he hadn't told him the whole truth about the hike.

He could hear Amber and Wes walking behind him and whispering to one another. He wanted to turn around and yell at them. Instead, he began replaying Wes's words in his head: *It was two to one, Jake. Two to one. So much for being a team.*

When they arrived back at the Sand Ramp Trail, Amber studied the ground to see if any boot prints might indicate the direction the Twin Owls had gone, but there were too many now, all pressed on top of one another. The kids looked to the north and then to the south, scanning the path for two men carrying a bright blue bag. But they didn't see a soul on the trail.

Amber decided to break the silence. "Jake, I know we're in a hurry, but we should talk about this."

"There's nothing to talk about." His mumbled response was barely audible.

"What did you say?" Amber asked.

"I *said*," he raised his voice, "that there's *nothing* to talk about."

"Well, obviously there is," she replied, "because you're still angry."

"We're wasting time." Jake started walking again. "We can talk about it later."

Jake's walk became a jog, and Amber and Wes kept pace with him without saying a word. Soon they came to the rise near Heavenly Valley. From there, they could look down onto an entire mile of the trail. Using their hands to shield their eyes, they studied the landscape. Again, the Twin Owls were nowhere in sight.

But something had caught Wes's attention, so he rummaged through his backpack and pulled out the binoculars. "Hey, guys," he called out. "Check this out."

He handed the binoculars to Amber, who looked, then passed them to Jake. Through the lenses, they could make out a few dark and hazy specks bobbing on the horizon.

"It's people," Wes said. "More than two, so it's not the Twin Owls. I bet that's part of the search-and-rescue team."

"If so, they're pretty fast," Amber mused. She looked

at her watch. "It's been about an hour and a half since we started hiking back."

"Let's run!" Wes bolted down the trail, followed by Amber and Jake. The closer they got, the pit in Jake's stomach grew tighter. *What would the search and rescue team think when they learned this emergency wasn't really an emergency? And when they realized they had dropped everything to find three kids who weren't really hurt or lost?*

About fifteen minutes later, they reached the group. A man about their parents' age approached them. "Are you the ones who called for help?"

Jake stepped forward. "We are. We're all okay. We weren't lost. It's just that we found the artifacts and watched two guys take them."

"Artifacts?" The man's brow wrinkled in confusion.

A young woman who was part of the team spoke up. "I talked to an NPS ranger this morning. He said that last night, looters ran off with some artifacts they'd discovered here in the dunes."

The man's eyes widened with surprise. "I'll call it in." He pulled the radio from his belt and began talking into it.

"Which way did the two men go?" the woman asked.

"We're not sure," Jake answered, still breathing heavily. "But if you didn't pass them, then they probably went north to the Liberty Gate."

"Kent," the woman called to the man with the radio,

"tell them that the men likely are headed for the Liberty Gate."

He nodded and relayed the information.

"Can you describe them?" she asked.

"Yeah," Amber answered. "They were like around our dads' ages and wore dark pants and had dress shirts on—like business clothing."

"How about their faces?"

Wes answered this time, "No, they were too far away and wearing sunglasses. But they're carrying a really big blue bag." He stretched out his arms, attempting to show them its size. "You can't miss that."

The woman gave the description to Kent, who again passed it on to the person on the other end of the radio.

"So, you haven't seen them?" Wes asked.

"We passed an older couple hiking, but that's it." The woman scratched the side of her head and studied the kids. "Are you three sure you're okay?"

The kids nodded. The woman dug into her pack and pulled out a candy bar for each of them. "You look exhausted. These should help."

Jake was relieved that she was more concerned than annoyed. In fact, the entire search-and-rescue team was happy and excited to have found the kids.

The man put his radio back on his belt and turned to talk with the kids. "They're sending a ranger over to the campground to let your parents know that you're all okay. I told them we'd hike out with you. I have to say, it sounds like they've been real worried about you kids."

Jake gave Amber and Wes an I-told-you-so look. Without words, they got the point.

An hour later, as they neared the trailhead, Jake spotted Uncle Brian hiking toward them. His stride was determined and fast. When they met, he examined them from head to toe. His uncle wasn't the sort of person who angered easily, but distress radiated from his skin like a sunburn.

"First, are you three *really* okay?" His voice was thick with concern and measured.

They all nodded, not yet saying a word.

"Then how did you get lost?" he asked.

"No, we didn't," Jake answered. He hated the idea of his uncle thinking that they got lost.

Uncle Brian pulled at the edge of his red beard. "Then please explain to me *why* you engaged the beacon."

Wes spoke up. "I did it. I hit the button."

"No, Wes," Amber broke in. "You and I agreed to do it. Jake didn't want to."

Jake and Ambers' eyes met, and he could feel his anger lighten. But part of him didn't want to let it go. *Two to one,* he recycled the words in his head.

Wes went on to explain how they had found the looters' stash, about the two men who had taken it, and why they decided to use the beacon, thinking it might help the rangers catch them.

"Well, I hope it works," Uncle Brian said. "But I was most concerned about you three." He gathered Wes into a big bear hug that lifted his feet off the ground. Jake could see his cousin's cheeks turning red with embarrassment.

Uncle Brian set Wes down. Then he leaned forward, putting his hands on his knees. He looked them each in the eyes. "I'm finding it hard to believe that you just *happened* upon the looters' stash."

Jake's insides knotted. *Please don't be mad*, he thought. He met his uncle's stare. "We thought it might be somewhere along the Sand Ramp trail." He stared down at his boots. "That's why we went. I'm sorry we didn't tell you."

Uncle Brian stood there, not saying a word.

"Are you going to stop us from exploring on our own?" Jake knew his uncle's decision would sway the rest of the parents. He'd spent more time in the wilderness than the rest of them combined.

"Maybe I should." Uncle Brian massaged his neck and shoulder like he was trying to work out the stress he'd been carrying.

Jake held his breath.

"No, I'm not going to suggest that," his uncle said.

"You kids did the right thing by using the beacon. But I am going to insist that from now on, you tell me the *whole* plan—not just parts of it."

The kids nodded. All the muscles in Jake's body relaxed as he let out a sigh of relief. He felt like a deflated balloon.

Uncle Brian turned to the search-and-rescue team. "I want to thank you—all of you—for responding and helping to find these three."

"You're welcome," Kent replied. "We're just glad they're okay and that we found them so quickly. In fact, they kinda found us."

Uncle Brian shook hands with everyone on the team, and the kids did, too. After expressing their gratitude, they headed back to the jeep.

"Let's get you all to camp so that you can clean up." He took their three packs from them and slung them over his shoulder. "I'm sure glad I took the doors and top off of the jeep." Uncle Brian playfully waved his free hand in front of his nose. Because, you three smell like a bunch of sweaty teenagers."

As the jeep pulled into the campground, Jake noticed two park service trucks near their campsites. Uncle Brian parked the jeep, and their parents came running out to meet them.

Jake's mom grabbed his shoulders and pulled him close for a hug. Her lips quivered as she spoke. "You had us so scared."

"Sorry that we scared you guys," Jake said. "We're all okay."

"We'd already heard," his mom replied. "Ranger Trujillo was here when the search-and-rescue team radioed in that they'd found you."

It was then that Jake heard a voice he didn't recognize. He looked over to see a woman talking to his dad. Her gray ball cap shielded her eyes from the sun. Over her matching ranger shirt, she wore a green vest that read: Police Federal Agent. He noticed a gun strapped to the holster on her belt, right next to her radio. From the sound of her voice and the way she talked, he guessed she was about the same age as his mom.

"We need to introduce someone to you." His mom gestured toward the woman.

"You must be Jake." The woman held out her hand.

He took her hand, surprised by the strength of her grip when they shook hands. "Are you the detective Ranger Trujillo was telling us about?"

"I sure am. My name is Agent Colter." Her voice was kind but serious. "It sounds like you and your friends have had an exciting twenty-four hours."

"It *has* been kind of crazy," Jake replied. He beckoned Wes and Amber over to join them. Then, he told Agent Colter about how they found the bag and opened it to discover the artifacts inside. He also told her about the two men who had taken it.

"The men were carrying a GPS unit that they used to locate the bag," he explained. "Inside, we found this." He pulled the crumpled piece of paper from his back pocket. "It looks like it's some kind of code."

Agent Colter took the paper and read it, mouthing the words under her breath: *This bag is one of three. I want ten times your original price. 13000604 Fatal Plazas.*

She looked up from the paper. "I'm sure you three kids are tired, but would you mind coming with Ranger Trujillo and me?"

"Are we in trouble?" Wes asked.

"No, we have the two hikers you kids saw last night at the pond and then again at the Liberty Gate. I'd like for you to listen in on a conversation with them. Perhaps the three of you can help us piece together this puzzle."

CHAPTER 15

1880 - Up Marble Mountain

Though cut and bruised, the dog was full of energy. He seemed, by instinct, to know exactly where he was going. Trusting the horses to follow him, he never ran too far ahead. If they fell behind, he'd stop and wait for them to catch up.

The dog sniffed his way along the narrow road that followed Medano Creek, the same one Emma and Gideon had taken the day before. He led them all the way up to Medano Pass, where a small cabin was tucked into a stand of spruce trees. Gray smoke curled from its chimney. The dog circled the cabin, sniffing the ground like he had picked up the scent for which he had been searching. Mr. Herard dismounted and tied his horse's reins to a hitching post. However, Emma stayed in the saddle with her eyes fixed on the dog.

As Mr. Herard approached the cabin, the door opened to reveal a man in his early thirties, clean-shaven, except for a brown mustache. His nightshirt was still crumpled, showing Emma that he must have hurriedly tucked it into his corduroy pants.

"Mr. Herard, sir. It's good to see you," the man said. "What brings you up my way so early in the morning?"

"Nice to see you, Gerald. Well, *that's* what brought us here." Mr. Herard pointed to the dog, who was completely preoccupied with the scent he had found. "Any chance you know who he belongs to?"

Gerald looked at the dog. "A few days ago, a young man came up the pass from the Wet Mountains. Not much older than Miss Emma." He nodded a greeting to her as he said her name. "He had a yeller dog like that one. But this one here looks moth-eaten compared to the one I seen with that boy."

"Which way did the boy go?" Mr. Herard asked.

Gerald pointed to the north. "He took to the ridgeline right through that way."

"Thank you, Gerald." They shook hands, and Mr. Herard untied his horse from the post.

He looked back at his friend. "If the young man shows up, let him know we have his dog. And if two shifty-eyed miners come asking about a dog—or that boy—pretend you never seen 'em."

"Will do, sir." Gerald nodded in respect and slipped his hands into the pockets of his trousers.

Mr. Herard got on his horse and headed north to the ridge. Emma followed and whistled to the dog. When they had traveled a few minutes along the faint ridge trail, the dog must have either picked up the scent or remembered the path because he took the lead again, steering them over the rocky mountainside.

They reached Music Pass at Noon. To their right, thousands of feet below the ridge, lay miles of flat grasslands, stretching east to the foot of the green and rolling peaks of the Wet Mountains. On the other side, Emma looked down into a forested mountain valley. But the dog continued straight ahead, working its way toward the summit of Marble Mountain. With every step, the ridge became steeper, and snow began to cover their path. Boot prints appeared in the snow. They had melted into icy tracks by the cycle of the warm sun and freezing nights. Then the dog stopped beside a massive gray rock outcropping. He began to pace nervously and whine.

But something else had captured Emma's attention. She slid out of Gideon's saddle and made her way toward something red that had been painted onto the side of the rock. She traced its contours with her fingers. A crimson Maltese cross.

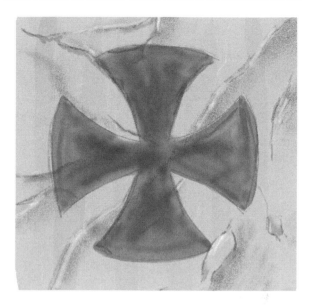

Looking back over her shoulder, she saw the dog approach a dark gap in the rock. Then he disappeared into the side of the mountain. Shocked, she turned around and approached what looked to be a mineshaft or perhaps a cave. The dog had been nearly silent the entire trip. But now, his distant barks and whines echoed in the darkness of the tunnel.

CHAPTER 16

THE INTERROGATION

Ten minutes later, the rangers' truck pulled up to a makeshift police station that had been set up behind the park offices. The three kids followed Agent Colter into one side of a large, vinyl, pop-up tent. A thick, plastic barrier divided the tent into two separate rooms. From their side, the kids could hear the muted sound of voices in the other room. Set into the barrier wall was a silver-tinted, plastic window. Jake gazed through it and immediately recognized the young woman and man who they had seen last night at the Liberty Gate.

"Don't worry," Agent Colter said in a hushed voice. "They can't see you." She tapped lightly on the silver-tinted plastic. "It's a one-way window. Those two have no idea that you kids even exist. And it's our job to keep it that way." She stepped toward the makeshift door. "Ranger Trujillo and I are going to ask them some questions I'd like for you guys to listen in. I'm hoping something they say will help us figure out what's going on."

"Okay," Jake said, as Wes and Amber nodded.

"If you talk, keep it to a whisper, okay." Agent Colter left, and a second later, they saw her enter the tent on the other side of the barrier. She sat down in a chair across from the two suspects, and Ranger Trujillo planted himself in the chair next to her. The young woman in pigtails was wringing her hands, and the young man with the short-trimmed beard kept fidgeting in his seat.

Agent Colter's voice was calm and strong. "We have evidence that you both stole archeological and cultural artifacts from federal lands in violation of the Archaeological Resources Protection Act. We also have reason to believe you have disturbed and possibly destroyed an archeological site."

She paused to let her words sink in. "These are serious crimes. We also know there was a third party involved who is likely in possession of the artifacts. Your cooperation is imperative and in your own best interest."

The young man cast a furtive glance at the girl like he was waiting for her to say something first. Then he blurted out, "His name's Jeff Claymont."

Agent Colter raised her eyebrows. "And..."

"And...and...," the man stammered, "... he's an assistant researcher at the university. Jeff told us that he got a call from someone who would pay us ten thousand dollars apiece if we would retrieve some artifacts from a pond in the dunes. He's been using a drone at night to scan the area. That's how he located it."

Agent Colter jotted something down on her notepad and then looked up. "Where is Mr. Claymont now?"

The young woman ran her fingernails along the top of her jeans as tears welled up in her eyes. Jake found himself feeling sorry for her, but Agent Colter pressed the question. "This is going to go better for both—" she looked directly at the young woman— "if you talk."

"We don't know where he is," the woman answered. Tears streaked down her cheeks.

"What more do you know?" Agent Colter's face was expressionless as a stone.

The young woman took in a deep and shaky breath. "Just after we collected the items, we hiked north toward the mountains. We came to a creek, and Jeff stopped us. He said the job was done and that we would get paid in a couple of days. Then he took the bags—his and ours—and left. We haven't seen him since."

"Who was Jeff working for?" Agent Colter asked.

The looters shook their heads. "We have no idea," the young man replied, his voice barely audible.

From her vest pocket, Agent Colter pulled the paper the kids had found. She handed it to the woman, who took it uneasily. "This was found with one of your bags," Agent Colter told her. "Can you tell us what this means?"

The woman stared at it, and the man shifted in his seat to read it.

"Sounds like Jeff is holding out on the buyer," he said.

"Was there something you found that might give Mr. Claymont the notion that these artifacts were worth ten times what he was being paid?"

The young woman nodded and stifled a sob. "Yeah, we dug up something that surprised all of us."

Jake looked at Wes and Amber. Like him, they, too, were leaning in toward the plastic window. Wes's nose bumped the surface, causing the vinyl divider to move and the young man on the other side to jump. Amber snickered, then clapped a hand over her mouth to keep from laughing out loud. Jake put his finger to his lips and glared at both of them.

The young woman sniffled and continued, "It was getting dark, so we had turned on our headlamps. Then I saw something glimmering at the bottom of the pond. At first, I just thought it was the reflection of my light on the water, but when I reached down to make sure, I felt something hard and cold. I pulled it up; a large silver arrowhead about the size of my hand, with markings carved into it."

Jake's mind swirled. *Could it be the spearhead from the journal?* Then his mind went to the old wooden box that Jasper had given to him in Rocky Mountain National Park, the locked box with no key and no apparent way to open it. He had imagined the spearhead lay inside. *Then what's in the box?* He wondered.

"Jake!" Amber grabbed his shoulder and gave him a light shake, rousing him from his thoughts.

He blinked his eyes and shook his head. Wes stood beside him, frozen with his mouth agape.

"Did you hear that?" Amber whispered, "They found a silver arrowhead!"

"Yeah, I did." His eyes narrowed, and his voice grew grim. "And that Jeff guy has it."

"What do we tell her?" Wes asked.

Jake could tell that Agent Colter was finishing up her questioning. She would soon return to their side of the tent.

"Let's think about it," Jake said.

More than anything, he wished he knew what Grandpa would have wanted him to do. They were on the scavenger hunt he'd set for them, and he knew Grandpa would want him to do the right thing. But he wasn't sure what that was. Should he tell Agent Colter about the spearhead in the journal?

Amber was biting her lip and thinking. "What about the Twin Owls? I feel like it might be pretty important to tell her that we saw the same guys in Rocky Mountain."

"I don't know," Wes said. "That might get them asking us a bunch more questions. Or it would be the opposite, and they would just think we were crazy."

Jake stared down at his shoes, hoping that somehow he could untangle the knots inside his head. He looked up at Wes and Amber again. "I think we tell them," Jake replied. "At least some of it. We don't need to explain everything. We just say...".

His words were cut short when Agent Colter pulled back the tent flap and entered. Through the window, he could see Ranger Trujillo leading the looters away.

"Did you kids hear or remember anything that might help us with the case?" Colter asked.

Jake looked at Wes, whose face was as readable as a slab of stone. "Yes." Jake hesitated, then continued, "We think we saw the same guys at Rocky Mountain National Park just a few days ago."

Agent Colter's eyes scrunched in confusion. "You saw the *looters* in Rocky Mountain?"

"Oh, no, that's not what I meant," he answered. "I mean, the two guys who took the bag today."

Agent Colter had received the written description of

the men from the search-and-rescue team's radio conversation. "What makes you think they were the same men?"

"Because they were dressed funny—like not in hiking stuff but in business-type clothes. That's what made us notice them in Rocky Mountain. They just looked out of place."

"Could you describe their faces?"

"Not really," Jake said, biting his lip. "They both wore sunglasses, and we were hiding, so it was hard to see exactly what they looked like."

Amber snapped her fingers. "But we could hear them talking. Don't you guys remember? They said something about the person they worked for."

"Yeah, they did." Wes pinched his lips with his fingers and then let go. "What did they call him?"

"The Director," Jake answered.

Agent Colter pulled the pen from her pocket and jotted something down in her notebook. "Anything else?"

The three of them shook their heads.

"Okay, guys," Agent Colter said, "You all have been a big help today." She tore out a sheet from her notepad and handed it to Jake. "This is my cell number. If you think of *anything* else, call me."

He took the paper, folded it, and put it in his pocket. "Did the two guys ever show up at the Liberty Gate?"

"There's been no sign of them." Agent Colter walked

over to the tent flap and held it open for the kids to exit. They stepped into the light of the setting sun to see Ranger Trujillo leaning against his truck.

"Let's get you all back to camp." He patted Jake on the shoulder. "You kids have got to be starving."

Chapter 17

The End of a Long Day

"I can't tell if I'm more tired or more hungry." Wes pressed his fork into the flakey crust of his pot pie, and steam billowed out. He breathed in the aroma. "Okay, I'm more hungry."

The sun had set, so Jake's dad placed a lantern on the picnic table where the kids were having dinner. Their parents had already eaten and were gathered around the campfire.

Jake had grown quiet. In fact, he hadn't spoken since their conversation with Agent Colter in the tent.

Amber noticed. "What's up, Jake? Is something wrong?"

"I'm just tired." He poked at his dinner.

"It sounds like you're more than just tired." She stared

at him, waiting for an answer. "Are you still mad at us about the beacon?"

He sighed, and his shoulders slumped. "No, I'm not." He paused and thought about it. "Well, yeah, I guess I kinda' still am upset with you two. But that's not what's bugging me."

"What's bugging you then?" Amber asked.

"I just feel like...like... we're *losing*."

"Losing what?"

"The silver spearhead," he mumbled. "It's got to be the one from the journal. But now that stupid Jeff Claymont guy has it, and he's going to give it to the director."

"But Jake, *we* took the note." She set her fork down and placed both her hands on the table. "So, the Twin Owls and the Director have no idea that Jeff has the spearhead and those other two bags."

Wes raised a finger to talk, but he waited until he had finished chewing his food. "I kind of feel like we're spies who intercepted a secret message." His eyes gleamed in the glow of the lantern light. "But I'm getting confused. There are too many people." He got up, went to the RV, and came back with something in his hand. Plopping a notepad and pencil onto the table, he began writing.

"What are you doing," Jake asked.

"This." He pushed the pad across the table to Jake and Amber. "Is that right?"

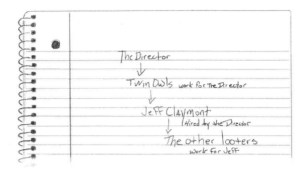

Jake took the pencil and added to the diagram. "Mather's note said THEY were after the box. I'm guessing that's The Director and the Twin Owls." He wrote THEY into the diagram.

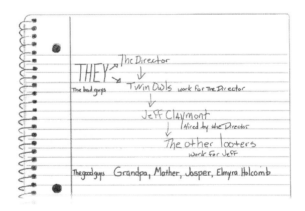

"How about Mather and Jasper?" Wes asked. "Where do they fit?"

Jake wrote them onto a separate line. "They were my

grandpa's friends. I'm guessing that this Elmyra Holcomb person was too." He wrote her name beside the others.

He slid the notepad back to Wes. "Even though we've got the note, the director will eventually figure it out." Jake leaned his elbow on the table and rested his chin in his hand. "He still has to pay Jeff. And when nobody show's up, Jeff is going to call him or email him or something."

"Maybe the rangers will catch him before that happens," Amber said. She picked up her fork and returned to eating her dinner.

"I guess," Jake breathed. "I just feel like I've messed this all up somehow. We've only got one more day, then we leave—and without the spearhead."

This time, Wes didn't wait to finish chewing. He muttered something that sounded like: "Ah dunt think tha sperrd as tha thig wereftr."

Jake looked at his cousin with wrinkled eyebrows and a slight shake of his head.

Wes swallowed his food and then repeated himself. "I don't think the spearhead is the clue we're after."

"What do you mean?" Jake asked.

"It's simple. Your grandpa didn't give us clues about the spearhead. Remember, he gave us a riddle about the pictures: *click, click, click.*" Wes shrugged, turning both his palms up like he was offering something obvious to Jake. "The silver spearhead drawing is *in the journal* we found in

Rocky Mountain National." He paused, then continued. "I'm not saying that it's unimportant. I'm just saying that it's not the clue your grandpa wanted us to find while we were at the Sand Dunes."

Wes grabbed his pencil and began writing more notes.

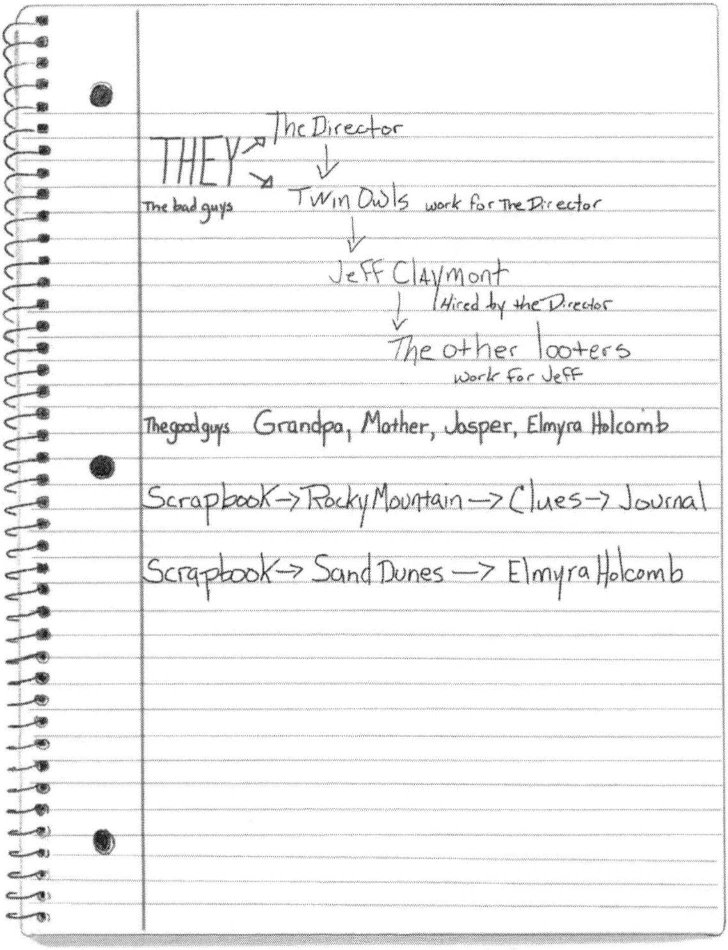

Handwritten notebook page:

THEY → The Director

The bad guys → Twin Owls   work for The Director

↓

Jeff Claymont
| Hired by the Director
↓
The other looters
work for Jeff

The good guys   Grandpa, Mother, Josper, Elmyra Holcomb

Scrapbook → Rocky Mountain → Clues → Journal

Scrapbook → Sand Dunes → Elmyra Holcomb

"I think Wes is right. Your grandpa gave us *two* clues in the scrapbook," Amber said. "*Elmyra Holcomb*, who we get to see tomorrow. And *Caverna Del Oro*..."

"A cavern that is like twenty miles away in the mountains—" Jake huffed in frustration—"and we'd have to hire a professional team of cave people if we wanted to go in there."

Wes snickered.

"What?" Jake's eyebrows narrowed in annoyance.

"It's just that you said 'cave people,' and I imagined a bunch of cavemen with clubs and torches leading us into a cavern."

Amber stifled a laugh and looked up at Jake, who was not amused. "Spelunkers," she explained, trying to speak in a more serious tone. "That's what cave explorers are called."

Jake folded his arms tight to his chest and let a short breath out his nostrils. "We're running out of time."

Wes scraped the edges of his pot pie tin, gathering the last bits of his meal. "Remember what you told me about your grandpa?"

"What's that?"

"You said that he was really *fun*." Wes smiled. "When we were younger, you were always talking about how he did fun stuff with you. I was kinda jealous because my grandparents are pretty boring. I don't mean that in a bad way. They're nice and all, but they don't do cool stuff with me or go off on adventures like your Grandpa Evans did."

But this only made Jake feel worse.

"I'm not trying to make you feel bad. I know you miss him a lot since he died." Wes straightened up and leaned across the table. "What I'm trying to say is that he put this whole scavenger hunt together so that you could have an adventure. He didn't want you to feel all stressed out like this. He wanted you to *enjoy* it."

He thought about Wes's words, and as he did, memories began playing in his mind. He recalled how his grandpa always searched him out and found him after a basketball or soccer game to tell Jake what he had done well. Or how Grandpa was never disappointed when his team lost. Instead, he always had something encouraging to say. Maybe the scavenger hunt was the same? Maybe it wasn't about winning or losing, but about enjoying the adventure.

"Thanks, Wes." Jake's body relaxed, and he uncrossed his arms. "And I'm sorry, guys, for being so angry and stuff."

"Dnnt aplle-gaze," Wes muttered, his mouth again full of food.

"Apple gaze?" The edges of Jake's eyes crinkled with both confusion and amusement at his cousin's indiscernible words.

"Sorry." Wes wiped his mouth with a napkin. "Don't apologize. But, please, eat your dinner. I think you're just hangry."

"Hangry?" Amber shook her head. "Don't you mean *angry*?'

"No, I mean *hangry*. It's what my mom says when my dad's in a bad mood after he's forgotten to eat lunch." Wes pointed to Jake's dinner. "Seriously, you need to eat."

Jake looked at the dinner he had barely touched and took a bite.

"I was angry because we didn't make the beacon decision as a *team*." He looked at Wes. "When you said, 'It was two to one,' I felt like you guys basically pushed me out."

"I promise, Jake," Wes replied, "I really didn't mean it that way. But I'd sure feel the same as you, if that happened to me."

Jake could feel the last bit of anger drained away. "Thanks for saying that, Wes."

"Yeah, Jake, we really didn't mean to push you out," Amber added. "I think we were all just really stressed."

Jake nodded and smiled.

"So, back to the clues," Wes said. "Your grandpa wouldn't have sent us into a dangerous cave with a huge drop-off. There's got to be something else we're supposed to do with the *Caverna del Oro* clue."

"Maybe they go together. I mean, the two clues.

Maybe they're *one* clue." Amber tapped her fingers on the weathered gray wood of the picnic table. "Maybe we're supposed to ask Elmyra Holcomb about the Caverna del Oro."

Jake's eyebrows raised, as did Wes's.

In his excitement, Wes pointed his fork at Amber. "Amber, that just might be it!"

But Jake was staring over his cousin's shoulder through the boughs of the pinyon pines that glimmered in the light of the campfire. "I'm still confused about the spearhead, though."

"Me, too." Wes turned to look behind him. "What are you staring at?"

Jake shook his head and broke the trance. "Sorry, I was just thinking."

The night air was growing cooler. Amber crossed her arms and rubbed her shoulders to warm them up. She leaned in toward the center of the table. "Maybe it's *serendipity*."

"Serendipi-what?" Jake asked.

"Serendipity. It's when things come together in unexpected ways, like when something good happens that you didn't plan."

A sudden warmth spread through Jake's stomach. He didn't think it had anything to do with the chicken pot pie. "I remember my grandpa saying something about that kind of thing. He used to say: 'Sometimes, when you're doing the right thing, it's a magnet for good stuff to happen.'"

"Maybe that's what's happening." Wes shrugged. "Whatever's happening, it's pretty cool."

"It really is." Amber got up from the table. "It's so cool that I'm exhausted and ready to crash."

"Me, too." Jake gulped down the last bite of his pot pie and gathered the aluminum containers and napkins to throw them away.

Wes followed Jake and Amber toward the campfire, mumbling something to himself.

"What are you saying?" Jake asked.

"*13000604 Fatal Plazas.*" Wes repeated it out loud again three more times. "I'm trying to get it into my mind before I fall asleep."

"Why?"

"Because your brain works on stuff while you sleep. Sometimes, I wake up in the morning, and the answer just comes to me."

Jake smiled at his cousin. "You're so weird."

"Thanks," Wes replied. "I'll take that as a compliment."

CHAPTER 18

1880 - Caverna Del Oro

Mr. Herard followed Emma into the tunnel, steadying himself with one hand against the cold, gray rock. "Wouldn't you know that dog would lead us into a hole in the ground?" He turned around and began walking out of the shaft. "I'm goin' to fetch us some light. Follow me. We can't afford to go falling down into a pit and getting killed up here."

They mounted their horses and rode down to the tree-line. Taking a hatchet from his saddlebag, Mr. Herard cut two branches from a pine tree. Then he used the hatchet to split one end of the branches, pried the ends open, and pressed a slender pinecone into the top of each. Scraping pine resin from the sides of the tree, he coated the cones with the syrupy substance.

He handed one of the branches to Emma, and they

rode back to the tunnel entrance, where the dog was still pacing and whining. From a small metal container, Mr. Herard pulled a match, struck it, and touched it to the pinecones. They ignited immediately, and the flammable resin began to crackle and burn.

Emma carried her torch into the cave tunnel until the dog, which had been out in front of her, stopped and stood at the edge of a deep pit. She kicked gravel from the floor into the void and listened.

"Over a hundred feet—that's for certain." Mr. Herard stretched his torch overhead, and the light revealed a set of pulleys and ropes. Handing his torch to Emma, he grasped a line and began pulling. As the hoists creaked, something rose out of the darkness below. When it reached the top, she realized it was a small, wooden platform.

"I can lower ya down, if you want to go," Mr. Herard said.

Emma nodded, her eyes inspecting the rickety contraption. She leaned one torch against the stone wall for Mr. Herard and then stepped onto the platform. Her stomach muscles tightened as it swayed over the pit. She grabbed a loop of rope above her head to keep her balance. The dog immediately joined her and nestled against her legs. Mr. Herard slowly let out the rope, and Emma watched his face dim and disappear as the light of her torch descended into the chasm.

CHAPTER 19

ELMYRA HOLCOMB

The next morning, Jake woke to the sound of voices at the campsite. He could hear Amber and Wes talking with Ranger Trujillo. *Wait, Ranger Trujillo is already here?*

He hurried to change, brush his teeth, and pull a baseball cap over his unruly hair. He opened the camper door to see everyone squeezed into the benches of the picnic table. Ranger Trujillo had pulled up a camp chair and was enjoying a cup of coffee. Amber and Wes were finishing their breakfast.

"Jake!" Wes called out. "I figured it out!"

"You figured out the note?"

"Well, I figured out the first half. It was actually kind of easy. It's *today*."

"Today? What do you mean, 'today'?"

"I mean, the numbers were a date—and a time," Wes explained. "I kept thinking of it as one big number: thirteen million six-hundred and five. That's what was getting me all confused. But look at this." He pulled a field journal from his back pocket and wrote out the numbers with a pencil, putting a space between the two zeros: *1300 0604*. "When I woke up this morning, it just came to me—that the numbers were really in *two* sets. Then it was easy. 1300 is military time for 1 p.m., and 0604 is a date, June fourth."

"Wait, that's...*today*." Jake rubbed his eyes, still feeling like he was waking up.

"That's exactly what I said," Wes replied. "It's one o'clock *today.*"

"Now we just need to figure out where Fatal Plazas is," Ranger Trujillo added. "We've run it through the FBI databases—even international addresses—and there is no such place." He checked his watch and stood up. "But mystery or not, we best get going. We're supposed to be over at Miss Elmyra's at ten o'clock. And I would never be late for Miss Elmyra."

"I'll be right back." Jake ran to the camper, where he grabbed his backpack, a couple of breakfast bars, and his water bottle.

When he came out, Ranger Trujillo was thanking Mr. Catalina for the coffee. He let the parents know that he'd drop the kids off at the Zapata Falls picnic area around noon.

About twenty minutes later, Ranger Trujillo turned the truck off the paved highway onto a long gravel lane lined with tall cottonwood trees. Jake spotted an old house surrounded by several red barns. As they drove down the drive, the truck leaving a trail of dust behind them, Jake felt that familiar buzzing sensation in his chest, the one he experienced every time they were close to uncovering the meaning of a clue.

They all got out of the truck and followed Ranger Trujillo to the front door, which opened before he could knock. A woman whose weather-worn face contrasted with her white dress and mint-green collar stood in the doorway. Her long, gray hair was pulled back into a pony-tail, held in place by a hummingbird clip adorned with green and diamond-like gems that sparkled in the morning light. Though Ranger Trujillo had said she was ninety-one years old, there was something very young about Elmyra Holcomb. Jake could see it immediately in the lines along her eyes and the way the corners of her mouth turned up. These were the signs of happiness and contentment.

"Come in, young man." She reached out to Ranger Trujillo and gave him a hug before beckoning the kids. "You all can join me in the sitting room." She turned and made her way into the house.

They followed Miss Holcomb and Ranger Trujillo into a room that contained a large wingback chair and two small couches, all mint green. Like Miss Holcomb, the furniture looked like it was from a bygone era, yet felt fresh and new. The walls were decorated with framed black and white photographs of people who Jake assumed were relatives. Mrs. Holcomb sat in the chair, and the kids and Ranger Trujillo found places on the couches.

"Miss Elmyra, I'd like to introduce you to Jake, Amber, and Wes."

"It's very nice to meet you all," she said. "I hear that you'd like to know about *Caverna Del Oro*." She leaned forward when she mentioned the name of the place, like she was sharing a secret.

"Yes, ma'am," Jake replied.

"Well, I've been to the caver—once," she explained. "And I've never been down inside—just to the entrance— but I knew someone who did. That's now over a hundred years ago when she went exploring down there. If it's alright with you all, I'll tell you her story."

The three kids nodded, and Mrs. Holcomb began her tale:

"When I was growing up here in the valley, there was a ranch just over the rise. I'd work for the family doing cleaning and laundry and such. Miss Emma paid me quite well, which says a lot, because back then, times were tough for all of us. Well, Miss Emma and I became good friends. Eventually, she and her husband moved somewhere out East. But she'd come by and see me whenever they were back this way visiting."

Mrs. Holcomb paused and looked across the room to a small table set with a teapot and several teacups. "Oh, I'm so sorry. I completely forgot the tea. Javier, would you be so kind as to serve us?"

"Certainly." Ranger Trujillo went to the table, poured tea, and handed the first cup to Mrs. Holcomb, and then he offered a cup to each of the kids.

Mrs. Holcomb took a sip and set her teacup and saucer on the side table. Folding her arms, she looked at the ranger with a proud smile. "Ranger Trujillo, as you know him, grew up running around this farm with my grandson. He's practically family." She paused again. "Okay, where was I?"

"You said that Miss Emma would come and visit," Jake replied.

"Oh, yes, thank you, Jake. So, during one visit when

she was gettin' on in years, she told me about how she'd found an injured dog up on the mountain." Elmyra pointed a shaky finger toward the window on the east side of the room. "Miss Emma was young then—just a few years older than you kids. After she nursed the dog back to health, it led her up through the mountains to a cave. Nearby a red Maltese cross was painted on the rock. If the legends are true, that's how the conquistadors marked the site of the *Caverna Del Oro*. Miss Emma said the dog ran right into the entrance, then got to whining and barking until she followed.

"But that cave is dangerous. I've been to that very spot, and I can tell you that the first drop would kill ya. Miss Emma said that there were animal bones scattered around at the bottom, evidence that some creatures hadn't been so careful. And that's why that dog was barking. He was smart and knew he couldn't go further without some help.

"Well, a local settler, Mr. Ulysses Herard—who was Miss Emma's guardian at the time—was with her. He made torches. And he figured out a way to lower her down, along with the dog."

Jake's eyes glimmered with wonder. He knew for certain this was the story his grandfather had intended for him to hear.

CHAPTER 20

1880 - WHAT EMMA FOUND

At the bottom of the cave, Emma found herself in a long, wide passage. There were boxes of tools and supplies along the walls. Boot prints were stamped into the dust on the floor. The dog began sniffing everything in sight. Catching a scent, they followed it deeper into the cavern. Emma looked up at her torch, hoping it would last long enough for the dog to find what he was looking for.

The cavern was made of countless branching paths and chambers. Every time a passage split, the dog's nose immediately told him where to turn. Emma tried to memorize their route, repeating it back to herself, "Right, left, left, right, left...". But while thinking about how she would have to reverse everything on the way back, she lost track of the list she had worked so hard to build in her head. Her breathing grew shallow as fear crept into her body like the cold chill which had already numbed her fingers and toes.

After another narrow passage, she and the dog stepped into an enormous chamber. Emma lifted the torch overhead and spun around to take in the size of the space.

"Our whole barn would fit in here," she breathed. Her words echoed off the chamber walls.

The torchlight caught a glint of metal on the far wall. As Emma approached, she could make out two wooden doors fixed to the wall with thick steel hinges. She pulled at a metal ring on one of the doors, and it groaned as it swung open. The dog bolted through. Inside was a smaller chamber that looked like a workroom. Wooden crates were stacked from the floor to the ceiling. There were trunks with padlocks and a long table where unlit lanterns hung overhead. Gold dust sparkled along the floor. And in the corner, sitting on the floor, and chained to the wall, was the slumped form of a young man. Emma gasped.

The dog licked the boy's face, shaking from nose to tail with excitement. The boy reached out and pulled the dog close.

"Thunder! You found me!"

He looked up to see Emma holding the torch. "I don't know who you are, but thank you. I was sure I was going to die down here."

Her arm trembled, still surprised by the sight of the

boy. "I'm Emma. But you should really be thanking your dog. He's the one that brought us here." She knelt beside him, holding the torch overhead and studying the shackles on his wrists. "Is there a key to these somewhere?"

"There are some bins of tools in the corner. I think that's where they put it."

Emma got up and rummaged through the metal bins until she pulled out a thick, heavy screw key. She twisted the key into the side of one of the shackles until it clicked open. She did the same with the other. The chain and shackles fell to the floor with a clank. Emma watched the boy as he tried to stand up.

"I think that I'm going to need your help," he groaned.

She slid her right arm under his armpit and worked to pull him to his feet. His weakened body shook as she attempted to steady him.

"I haven't stood straight or eaten for days. At least, I think it's been days. It's hard to tell down here in the dark. But if I can move a bit, I think that I'll be okay."

He rested his hand on a crate. Emma stood back and watched as he took a few cautious steps.

"Why did they lock you up?"

"It's a long story." He looked around the room. "I'll tell you when we're safe. First, we need to get out of here before they come back."

She nodded and headed for the door.

"Wait, just one thing. Can I use your torch?"

"Sure." She handed it to the boy.

With the light in hand, he hobbled across the room to the oak doors. The boy began feeling the rock, running his fingers along each stone, then he stopped. Emma knelt beside him as his fingers traced something carved into the rock, another Maltese cross. He jiggled the stone, loosening it from the wall, then pulled it free. He reached into the recess left by the stone, pulled something out, and pressed it into his pocket.

"Thanks." He handed the torch back to Emma, his arm shaking from being so weak.

They left the room and followed Thunder through the maze of cavern passages back to the platform. Emma shook her head in wonder at the dog, who retraced their steps without forgetting a thing. She looked up and could see the dull orange glimmer of Mr. Herard's torch above them.

"You should go first, Emma," the boy said.

"That's quite gentlemanly of you," she replied. "But I'll be just fine going up next with Thunder." She held the rope and steadied the platform. "By the way, I've given you my name, but you've not told me yours."

"Oh, sorry. Please, beg your pardon. I'm not exactly thinking straight. My name is Abraham, but you can call me Abe."

"It's a pleasure to meet you, Abe," she said. "Now, let's hoist you up out of here."

He sat on the platform, and Emma yelled up to Mr. Herard, "Pull!"

Soon Emma, Abe, and Thunder were standing in the warm sunlight outside the cave.

"I'd sure like to know why you were down inside the mountain, son," Mr. Herard said. "But I've got a feeling we best get outta here before them folks who captured you return."

From Gideon's saddlebag, Emma drew a canteen and handed it to Abe, who gulped down every last drop. Mr. Herard brought his horse alongside them. "Abe, you're in no shape to go on foot, so take my horse. I'll walk."

They made their way back down the mountain, arriving at Medano Pass near sunset. Mr. Herard checked in with Gerald at the cabin and asked him to keep quiet about the young man and the dog. From Medano Pass, they took the road home. The light of a half-moon passed through the forest canopy, casting shadows across their path. Crickets and other summer bugs chorused in the night air. Gideon knew the way in the dark, so Emma spent the time wondering about the boy riding beside her.

A few hours later, through the pines, she spotted the warm glow of lanterns shining from the cabin's windows. Her body relaxed. They were home.

CHAPTER 21

THE LEGEND OF THE MOON PONDS

Mrs. Holcomb took another sip of tea. "That dog knew right where he was going."

Jake scooted forward to the edge of the couch. "So, did the dog really belong to the boy who was all chained up?"

"That's exactly right. The dog had led Miss Emma to his master—and her future husband."

"Wait." Wes scratched his head. "The guy in the cave was her husband?"

Mrs. Holcomb snickered a kind laugh. "Not yet," she explained. "Years later, however, she would marry that young man." Mrs. Holcomb laughed again. "Can you imagine that? Finding yourself a husband hidden away in a dark cave high up on a mountain. Sounds like a fairy tale, doesn't it?"

She leaned back into her chair, cradled her teacup in both hands, and sighed. "But you know, life, it turns out that way, but only when you really *live* it—when you go on adventures, take risks, and do courageous things like Miss Emma."

"Why was the boy chained up inside the cave?" Jake asked.

"Well, he was searching for something—actually, he was *recovering* something that had been stolen by a gang of folks who were operating out of that cavern. Whatever it was they had going on in that cave, nobody's been able to figure out. After he escaped, they emptied the place and even took those doors down. Explorers found an old hammer, some rotted rope, and a couple of other things. But it's like they just up and disappeared." Her eyes had a faraway look as though she was trying to see out beyond the walls of the room. After a moment of silence, she set her teacup back on its saucer and rested her hands on her legs. "Well, that's the story of *Caverna del Oro*. You were probably hoping I was going to tell you that there was still gold hidden up there somewhere. Hope you're not too disappointed."

The kids sat in silence for a moment. Then Ranger Trujillo interrupted the quiet. "Miss Elmyra, I think the kids would also like to hear the story of the moon ponds."

Her eyes gleamed as she sat up in her chair. "Yes. I've

heard one of the moon ponds returned and you three stumbled upon it."

"Just a couple of days ago," Amber explained. "We were sandboarding in the dunes and found one."

"Oh, you *must* go back and visit at night," Mrs. Holcomb said. "To see the stars reflecting on the water in the middle of the dunes. It feels like you could step into another world."

Mrs. Holcomb got a dreamy look in her eyes. "When I was just eight years old, I was out exploring the dunes with my papa, and we came upon a set of ponds—right out there in the middle of the yellow desert. To this day, I've never seen anything like it. We sat down, and papa told me a story he'd heard from an old trapper." She looked at the kids and raised her eyebrows. "Would you like to hear it?"

"You bet we would," Wes said. He had been leaning so far off the edge of the couch that he nearly slipped off.

Mrs. Holcomb closed her eyes. After searching her memory, she began, "A long time ago, the ancestors of the native tribes would come into this valley. Archeologists now call them the Clovis and the Folsom people, but nobody really knows their true names. They lived around these parts over ten thousand years ago. But the tale goes that a young warrior on a vision quest came wandering through the dunes in the middle of the night. He climbed to a high dune and saw a gleam of blue and silver in the distance. It was the first moon pond. Captivated by the sight, he made his way down to the water's edge.

"The moon shone brightly on its surface, but beneath the moon's reflection, the warrior noticed a glint of a brighter light. He stepped into the water, drawn by the glimmer at the bottom of the pond. Reaching in, he grasped the object and pulled out what he at first thought was a stone. But it was heavier than any rock of that size. It was pure silver.

"It wasn't alone. He saw another gleam in the water, reached in, and drew out a second piece of silver. He thanked the Creator, who he believed had given him two fallen stars.

"The warrior carried these with him as he wandered the land. Over the years, he grew wise. He understood how the rivers and mountains, canyons and clouds gave shape to the lives of the creatures of the earth and people. Some say he lived three lifetimes exploring the lands west of the great river. And in his old age, before he died, he fashioned the two pieces of silver into spear tips and carved his secrets into their surface."

The kids looked at each other, dumbstruck.

"Then, the warrior went on a final pilgrimage to lay the fallen stars to rest. One he planted in the heart of the sand dunes, and one he hid in the heart of the sky."

Jake rubbed his forehead, completely stunned. He

thought about the drawing of the silver spearhead in his great-great-grandfather's journal, the one they had found in Rocky Mountain National Park. *He carved his secrets into their surface. The spearheads are like the scrapbook.* He thought. *The markings mean something. That's why they're so valuable. It's not the silver—it's the secrets. And that's why the director is after them.*

Ranger Trujillo checked his watch. "Miss Elmyra, thank you for the stories. We should head out now. These kids are supposed to meet their parents for a picnic soon."

"Well, I'm so grateful for your visit," she replied.

The kids got up from the couches and expressed their gratitude to Mrs. Holcomb. They followed Ranger Trujillo back out to the truck. Jake, still overwhelmed by all he had just learned moved slower than the rest and was the last one at the door. He was about to step onto the porch when Mrs. Holcomb called out to him, "Jake Evans, I have something for you."

Surprised, he whirled around and walked back into the sitting room. "How did you know my last name?" he asked.

She looked at him, and Jake could tell she was taking him all in, from the bottom of his sneakers to the top of his brown head of hair. "I knew who you were the minute you walked through that door," she said. "You have Miss

Emma's eyes, and you're the spittin' image of Abraham Evans."

"You mean...the boy she found in the cavern was related to me? Was he my...? And Emma was my..?"

"Yes." Mrs. Holcomb's brimmed with delight. "What would that make them? Your great-great-grandparents?"

So full of wonder, he could barely breathe to talk. "Yes, Ma'am," he stammered.

"Miss Emma asked me to give you something," She walked over to an old roll-top desk and pulled up the front. With two hands, she tugged open a drawer and withdrew a leather pouch about the size of her hand. She walked with it back over to Jake, who was standing stock still, unable to take his eyes off her.

"She told me, that if one day a member of her family came to pay me a visit, and mentioned the Caverna del Oro, I was to give them *this*." She handed him the canvas bag.

He looked inside. "What is it?" he asked.

"It's something they found in *Caverna Del Oro*." She gave him a knowing smile. "I think this is what Abraham was searching for."

Jake took another, longer look into the pouch. Inside was a wooden cube, not much bigger than a golf ball.

"Miss Emma told me to keep it hidden." Elmyra patted him on the shoulder. "The men who chained her husband up in that cavern valued this strange thing more than their bars of gold. And she said to expect them to come looking for it."

He pulled a wooden cube from the bag and held it in his hands.

"Then, this past September, I got a phone call from someone claiming to be Miss Emma's grandson."

"My Grandpa Evans?"

Mrs. Holcomb nodded. "He'd planned to travel out this way to meet me and pick up the object. Said it was some sort of map."

Jake turned the cube over, examining its surface. *Doesn't look anything like a map.*

"Then he called a couple of weeks later to tell me of his diagnosis." She placed her hand gently on his shoulder. "I'm sorry, Jake. He seemed like a good man, and a wonderful grandfather."

Both sadness and wonder welled up in his chest. Hand trembling, he put the cube back into its leather pouch, and then put the pouch into his backpack. "Thank you, Mrs. Holcomb. I really miss him."

"I bet you do." Her kind eyes were filled with understanding, an understanding forged from much love and many losses. She gazed out the window to where the others stood, waiting for Jake. "Now, you should get going to that picnic."

He turned and started for the door, but he stopped when she called out his name one more time. "Jake," she said, "folks looking for treasure often forget themselves, and they forget what they're really after."

"What's that?" he asked.

"You've got to figure that one out for yourself. That's the real treasure hunt."

They smiled at each other, and he wondered if she was looking at him or if she was grinning at the memory of her friends, Emma and Abe Evans. In that moment, he could feel their blood pulsing through his veins. The whole world seemed to be expanding, and he was captured by a sense that he was now living a story that was much bigger than himself.

"Thank you," he said, and then he opened the screen door, and ran across the yard to the truck.

CHAPTER 22

AT THE WATERFALL

They drove out the long lane and turned onto a narrow, gray road surrounded by miles and miles of green pastures. Wes, in the front passenger seat, pointed to a group of cattle grazing in one of the distant fields. He said something to Ranger Trujillo that Jake couldn't understand over the wind racing through the open windows.

From the back seat beside him, Amber leaned forward to look, her brown and purple-streaked hair fluttering behind her. She turned back to Jake. "It's elk."

A herd of what looked like over one hundred elk grazed alongside the cattle. Ranger Trujillo tapped Wes's shoulder and pointed up ahead to where another group of massive brown animals was moving through a sea of yellow and green meadow grass. As the truck got closer, the kids could see that it was a herd of bison. Three of the bison calves had gathered to play what looked like a game of chicken. One would charge and send the other two off, kicking up dust and bucking.

Talking as loudly as he could so the kids could hear him, Ranger Trujillo explained, "The bison give birth in the spring, so most of these little ones are just over a month old."

A few moments later, he gestured out the window again. "Keep your eyes peeled for pronghorn."

"What did he say?" Jake asked Amber. Between the thrum of the diesel engine and the reverberations of the wind, it was almost impossible to hear what anyone was saying in the front seats.

"To look for pronghorn," Amber replied.

"Pronghorn?" Jake asked.

Wes turned around and yelled back, "It's a kind of antelope that live out here."

Jake nodded and kept studying the landscape for more animals. They were only a few miles further down the road when Amber pointed out her window at a herd of animals that resembled deer. Some had dark, black horns that looked like someone had buffed them with shoe polish. Their ebony surface gleamed in the sunlight. Unlike deer antlers that branched out and up, these were smaller, curved in, and hooked back behind their heads.

"It's the pronghorn!" Wes called back.

As Ranger Trujillo started to talk, Jake and Amber tugged at their seat belts and leaned forward between the front seats so they could hear.

"Both deer and elk have antlers. It's bone that grows right out of their skulls. But those pronghorn—and the bison—grow *horns*, which aren't bone at all. It's something more like what your fingernails are made out of."

Jake sat back and took it all in. What looked like a desert and flat grasslands—something he would have first thought to be boring—was instead teeming with life.

Cattle, elk, bison, pronghorn. He wondered what else might be out there creeping in the grass.

Soon they came to a big, brown forest service sign that read: *Zapata Falls Recreation Area.* Ranger Trujillo slowed the truck and turned left onto the gravel road. They were driving toward the mountains now, and in front of them, three snow-covered peaks rose into the sky.

"You kids came at the perfect time," Ranger Trujillo said. "With the heat and all that snow, the waterfall is going to be gushing."

A few miles up the winding road, he pulled the truck into a parking lot where the kids could see their parents setting out lunch on picnic tables. Ranger Trujillo parked the truck, and they all got out.

"Ranger Trujillo," Jake's dad called out, "how about you join us for lunch?"

He reached out his hand, and Ranger Trujillo took it.

"Thank you. I am due for a lunch break."

"Do you really ever take a break?" Jake's dad asked.

"Not really. Out here, I'm always on duty. But it's a good life."

As usual, the kids found their own picnic table and sat down to eat together. Wes was staring over Jake's shoulder at something behind him. Jake turned around to look but saw only the dirt road and a grove of stunted pinyon pines.

"What are you thinking about?" Jake asked.

"The code." Wes wiped his mouth with a napkin and then placed it under his plate so that it wouldn't blow away. "You know that feeling you get when a word is on the tip of your tongue, but you just can't get it?"

"Yeah, I do. I hate that feeling."

"That's how I feel. Like my brain knows what the message means, but it won't tell me." Wes looked at Amber's watch. "And it's twelve-thirty already." He grunted with frustration.

"Yeah, even if we figured it out now, it's probably too late to do anything about it," Jake replied.

Amber, who had been quiet during lunch, got up to throw away her plate. Before returning, she stopped to talk with her parents and Uncle Brian. When she finished the conversation, she walked back over to the boys.

"Our parents are okay with us going to the waterfall. It's just a short hike that way." She pointed across the gravel parking lot toward a grove of aspen trees.

"Cool," Jake replied and began scarfing down the rest of his lunch.

He and Wes threw away their plates, grabbed their daypacks, and began walking with Amber toward the trailhead.

"You guys got plenty of water?" Uncle Brian called out.

Wes gave his dad a thumbs up.

The trail was rugged but easy and short compared to yesterday's adventure on the Sand Ramp Trail. The path led to a shallow creek flowing out of a rocky ravine. They took off their shoes and socks and walked through the clear waters of the creek and into the narrow gorge.

"This reminds me of the crevice at Twin Owls," Amber said.

"Yeah, it sure does. But I like it better," Wes replied. "I don't feel claustrophobic like I did in there."

Jake could hear the murmur of falling water in the distance. Cold water chilled the skin from his toes up to his shins. As they walked, the placid creek narrowed, creating a current that required him to plant his feet into the coarse sand to keep from slipping. Overhead, the sides of the ravine joined to form a rugged stone ceiling. A crack snaked through it, revealing occasional slivers of blue sky.

As the current grew stronger, the water rose to their knees, and a rumbling echoed off the now moss-covered rock walls. They came around a bend, and there in front of them was the strangest waterfall Jake had ever seen. It fell through a stone chute and plunged down into a large rock-walled chamber. Hitting the wall, it appeared to bounce back and crash into a second, smaller waterfall. Then its waters tumbled over rocky cascades and into the pool that now surrounded them and soaked their legs.

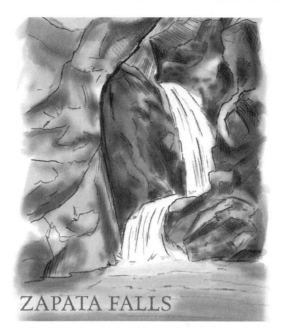

ZAPATA FALLS

Jake was captivated by the sight. Then, he felt Amber's elbow jab him in the ribs.

"What is it?" Jake asked.

She didn't answer. Instead, she shot her eyes to the right. They weren't alone. Just behind them, near the back wall of the chamber, a man stood looking at his watch, his arms and face grimy with dust and dirt. He wore a blue hat and had pulled his long, brown hair back into a ponytail. Jake's heart began to beat out of his chest. It was the third looter, Jeff Claymont.

Wes was still staring up at the waterfall when Jake

reached forward and tapped him on the shoulder. He turned around, saw the man, and jumped. He looked at Jake and Amber; his eyebrows arched high on his forehead as if to ask without words, *what do we do now*? Jake put his finger to his lips. He motioned for them to head out of the chamber and back toward the trail.

They didn't say a word until they were out of the ravine and had stepped from the water onto the sandy edge of the creek.

"Are we sure that's him?" Amber asked.

"It's got to be," Jake replied. "I mean, it was getting dark when we saw him the other night, but he had a ponytail and a blue hat—just like the one that guy is wearing."

"*Auauauaughghghgh*," Wes moaned and held his head in his hands.

"What's wrong?" Amber asked.

"That's it! Look." Wes picked up a stick and drew in the sand, Fatal Plazas. "It's like a word scramble. Unscrambled, it spells *Zapata Falls*."

"That's why it was on the tip of your tongue," Amber said. "Because we've been seeing it on signs and saying the words all morning." She checked her watch. "It's one-fifteen right now. Soon, he's going to realize that the Twin Owls aren't going to show up."

"We need a plan," Jake said. "Wes, how about you run

back to get Ranger Trujillo? Amber and I will stay here to keep an eye on Jeff Claymont."

"Sounds good," Wes replied.

They scrambled to put on their socks and shoes. Then Wes took off running down the trail.

CHAPTER 23

ON THE HILLSIDE

No sooner had Wes disappeared than Jeff Claymont came walking out of the gorge toward them. Jake and Amber froze. Then Amber whispered, "Just act normal and keep tying your shoes." They could hear Jeff's shoes leave the water and crunch on the gravel beside them. Without pausing, he glanced at the kids, nodded an uninterested greeting, and then walked past them.

They held their breath. After Claymont passed, they let out exhales of relief.

"I keep forgetting that he has no idea we even exist," Jake whispered. He stood up, offered Amber his hand, and pulled her to her feet.

They watched as Jeff Claymont continued down the

trail and turned left onto a faint path that weaved through the trees and up to the area above the ravine.

When he was out of earshot, Jake turned to Amber. "I bet he has the artifacts stashed somewhere up there. Let's follow him."

The side trail was steep, wooded, and rocky. On their left, they could see the edge of the gorge, lined by jagged rock spires that had crumbled into the woods. The sound of falling water rumbled far below. As the trees started to thin, the trail opened onto a broad, rounded ridge covered in short grasses and sagebrush. Across the ridge, Claymont was working his way up a steep hillside. Jake and Amber stopped in the cover of the trees and crouched low.

The slope was made of scree, penny-sized gravel that caused Claymont's boots to slide backward with each step. He slipped and slid a few feet down the slope. Jake could hear an indistinct curse word and watched as the looter struggled back up the hill. This slowed his progress, but he soon arrived at the base of a large, brown boulder. The massive rock was the size of a refrigerator and cast a long shadow down the slope. Twenty feet down from the boulder and directly in its path were two blue bags, just like the one they had found along the sand ramp trail.

"You were right," Amber whispered. "He's got the artifacts."

Jake leaned out to get a better view. "There's something tied to the top of the bags."

Amber squinted. "Yeah, they're straps, like the ones my dad uses to hold things down in the back of his truck."

Claymont pulled something out of his back pocket. A glint of silver flashed from the object.

"He's got the spearhead, too," Jake whispered.

Grabbing a shovel lying beside the boulder, Claymont threw it over his shoulder and trudged further up the hillside. Reaching the top of the hill, he kept walking until he disappeared into a stand of pine trees and aspens.

"I've got an idea," Jake said. "Stay here and wait until Wes can get help. I'm going to see if I can get those bags."

"I'm not going to just stay here hiding." Amber shook her head. "I'm going to follow him. I can sneak through the trees over there." She pointed to her right, where the open ridge dipped into a shallow, wooded gully that could provide her the cover needed to sneak up and keep an eye on Claymont. But Jake's route was completely exposed. If Claymont returned, Jake would have nowhere to hide.

His eyes met Amber's determined gaze. "Sounds good. Let's go."

Amber bolted across the open area at the bottom of the hill and disappeared into the gully. Jake dashed across the meadow. When he got to the hillside, his sprint slowed to a crawl as the scree kept slipping out from underneath his feet. The noise of gravel spilling down the slope behind him made Jake even more nervous. He tried to be more careful, planting one foot, pressing down, then placing his other foot above the first. This slowed his progress even more, but it was much quieter. Just a few more steps and he would be able to reach the bags.

A sound from the gully made him jump. He looked over his shoulder to see if he could spot Amber, but she was nowhere in sight. The quiet was unnerving. Pressing down on his right foot to take another step, Jake slipped in the loose gravel. He threw his body forward to keep from falling backward and slammed his chin into the ground. Wincing at the impact, he dug his fingers into the rock and dirt, trying to slow his slide down the hill. When he finally stopped, his arms and knees were red with scratches and scrapes. But that didn't matter. He had to get the artifacts.

Realizing the direct route was too precarious, he studied the ground for a better approach. The hillside to his right wasn't as steep, and the ground looked more stable. He scrambled up the slope again and was soon even with the bags, but they were still far to his left and out of reach. Just above the bags, Jake could see a dent in the ground where a scraggly sagebrush grew. The shallow depression might give him a level place to stand and reach down to grab them.

He took each step with care, praying the ground wouldn't give way again. Finally, he made it to the dent. He tugged on the gray trunk of the sagebrush to see if it might hold his weight. It did. Next, he pressed his foot into the ground, stretched out his free hand, and closed his fingers around the top of the nearest bag. It slumped toward Jake. Its black strap shot out from under the gravel and stretched taut. The other end of the strap was tied to a metal rod, driven into the ground at the base of the giant boulder.

Jake froze. It was a trap.

If he pulled on them, the metal rod holding the

boulder would pry loose and send the giant rock careening down the hill, crushing him in its path.

He let go of the bag and watched the black strap fall back onto the ground. That small movement was enough to break free a mass of loose gravel at the base of the boulder, sending a cascade of dirt and grit spilling down the hillside and into Jake's face. He spat the dust from his mouth and rubbed it away from around his eyes.

The dust cloud dispersed, and his eye's shot to the boulder. He sighed with relief. It hadn't moved, but the ground underneath it had begun to cave away.

Breathing hard, he scanned the hillside for signs of Claymont or Amber. He had to get away from the path of the boulder. Then, without warning, the sagebrush he was hanging onto tore out of the ground, and Jake went with it. He tumbled backward, hit the bags with his back, and slid downhill until something caught his ankle and whipped his body to a halt. Through the dust, he saw the black strap snap tight.

Jake looked uphill to see the strap wrapped around his ankle. His eyes immediately shot to the metal rod jammed under the boulder. It was bending. He crunched his stomach muscles, reached up to the strap, and tried to loosen its grip on his ankle. But it was too tight. He wished he had listened to Wes. Right now, he really needed a knife.

Another sound distracted him. This time it came from

the trees and brush on his left. Amber burst out of the thicket and crawled across the slope to Jake's side.

"Whoa, what happened?" she asked.

"Don't pull on the strap!"

Amber's eyes followed the black line from his ankle to the metal rod. Her eyes widened, then she looked back at Jake. "Okay, you've got to try to scoot yourself uphill to loosen the line." She paused and turned her eyes to the top of the hill. "We've got to hurry! Claymont is coming back."

"I'm trying," he grunted, pressing his arms against the ground and shuffling his legs uphill. More sand and gravel spilled down the slope into his face.

"That's it," she said. "Keep doing that."

Amber pulled Jake's shoe off to get it out of the way, loosened the strap, and slipped it off his ankle.

They heard a crunch and looked up to see the boulder shift. Jake clambered onto his hands and knees. One end of the boulder had moved several inches downhill, and more rock and dirt were crumbling out from underneath its weight. He tried to crawl toward the bags but stopped when he heard the sound of Claymont whistling. They scrambled back across the slope and hid in the brush at the edge of the forest. Amber handed Jake his shoe.

"Thank you," he whispered.

They watched as Claymont appeared on the hillside

above the boulder. He looked down at the bags that were now covered with dust and dirt. He looked at the boulder. His eyes narrowed, and he began looking around. Just then, a voice came from the meadow at the bottom of the hill.

"Hello!" The voice called out. "Sorry I'm late, Mr. Claymont."

An older man walked across the open ridge. He smoothed his white hair and put on a pair of aviator sunglasses as Claymont began working his way down the hill toward him. The man's white dress shirt and khaki pants made him look like he had just come for a business meeting. This was not some random hiker. In fact, both Jake and Amber thought the person seemed familiar. They crept through the brush and trees until they were close enough to hear the conversation.

"We had some problems getting your message, Jeff," the older man said. "Seems you got a bit careless."

"What do you mean?"

"I mean that you agreed to bring *all* the items to the drop point. Holding my property hostage wasn't the plan. Then your little ransom message got intercepted by some kids."

"I don't understand." Claymont rubbed the sweat from his forehead and eyebrows.

"They found your note while hiking, and passed it on

to the authorities. Luckily, one of your partners found out and sent me the message."

Claymont, who had been so confident, now looked nervous. He bit his lip and glanced around as if he were looking for somewhere to hide. Though he was much younger and stronger, there was something intimidating about the older man's presence.

"Your note demanded *ten times* the original price," the older man said. "Might I ask why?"

"Well, it's...because...." Claymont stammered, "I found something more...valuable than... I'd expected."

"But that wasn't the deal, Jeff," the older man said.

"The director told me that I'd get a fair price," Claymont replied.

"I *am* the *Director*," the man replied. "And *I'm* the one who sets the price."

Concealed in the undergrowth, Jake looked at Amber, his mouth open in amazement. Then he whispered, "That guy is *the director!*"

Amber nodded. "Listen, he's saying something again."

The director pointed up the hill at the blue bags and asked, "And what's *that* all about?"

"That's *leverage*." Claymont stood up straight again and pulled his shoulders back in what Jake assumed was an attempt to regain his confidence.

The director studied the boulder, the metal rod, the

straps, and the bags. "Oh, I see. Let me guess your rookie plan, Jeff. You expected my associates to show up here and refuse your demands. You knew you'd be outnumbered. Or that maybe one of my boys would come armed. So, you made yourself a little booby trap thinking that would guarantee the payment."

"That's about right." Claymont's voice sounded strong, but Jake could see that he refused to look at the director, who remained relaxed and confident. The looter was outmatched.

"This is unfortunate, Jeff. You came highly recommended. I had hoped we could use you on more jobs like this one. But you've gone and made a real mess of things for me." The director looked back over his shoulder like he was waiting for someone. Jake followed his eyes and studied the trees below the ridge, wondering if perhaps the Twin Owls were on standby.

The director turned back to Claymont. "I don't care about what's in those bags, Jeff."

Claymont appeared taken off guard. "What do you mean?"

"I know your type well enough," the director replied. "That thing you found in the dunes that you believe is so valuable, you wouldn't risk it getting destroyed. It's not in those bags."

Claymont's shoulders slumped, and his face became white. Any advantage he had was gone.

"You were right about one thing, Jeff. That artifact is what's valuable to me." The director stepped forward, his hands in his pockets. "So, here's the new deal. My associates are waiting down below. Like me, they're not very happy with you right now. So, you're going to fetch the item and bring it to me. Then I'm going to let you go, unpaid and unharmed."

Claymont pressed his hands in his pockets and stared at the ground. After a few moments of thought, he lifted his eyes, looked at the director, and muttered, "Okay. I'll go get it."

Just then, Jake heard a crunch from the top of the hill. He turned to see more rock and dirt crumble from underneath the boulder. It shifted. The metal rod bent. And the ground underneath the giant rock collapsed, setting it free to crush everything in its path.

CHAPTER 24

THE BOULDER

J ake burst out of the woods and ran toward the bags. What happened next spanned seconds, but he experienced it all in slow motion.

The boulder lurched forward like the giant wheel of a steamroller.

The metal rod bent under its weight before recoiling like a spring. It shot through the air.

The black straps followed, arcing through the sky.

Jake bolted toward them and caught hold of the straps as they fell.

The boulder began to rotate and roll.

He frantically yanked on the straps, hoping to pull the bags out of harm's way. But they were heavier than he'd expected. The boulder picked up speed. Jake threw the straps over his shoulder and strained against their weight. They moved only inches.

He could hear the crunch of earth as the boulder careened down the hillside. Its shadow engulfed the blue packs.

Jake ran, pulled, and jumped, hoping that the weight of his body might dislodge the bags. As he fell, the force wrenched them from the ground and into the air. The boulder grazed the nylon surface of the last bag as it went by.

He skidded across the gravel and dirt. It was like sliding across coarse sandpaper, scraping the skin of his forearms. His knees hit next. A shot of pain ran from his kneecaps down his legs and into his feet. He heard a howl of pain— but it wasn't his. Jake rolled backward down the steep slope, the straps wrapping themselves around his chest and legs until he came to a stop. Laying on the ground, he watched as the boulder hurtled down the hillside and crashed into the rocks at the bottom. The sound of the impact echoed off the surrounding mountains like the report of a gunshot. Dust filled the air around him. Silence.

Amber came running across the hillside. "Jake, are you alright?" She crouched down beside him.

Jake groaned. "Are the artifacts okay?"

"They're fine. You got them out of the way—just in

time."

He collapsed in relief. After taking a deep breath, he pressed up from the ground and worked to stand up. His right knee was bleeding, and his arms stung from long red abrasions. He shook loose from the straps, and they fell in a circle at his feet.

They both looked downhill to see the director standing over Claymont, who was holding his right leg and cursing. He had been in the path of the boulder and was lucky that it had caught only his leg. The director looked up at Jake. Though sunglasses hid his eyes, Jake could feel his patient and unrelenting stare.

Aware he'd been seen, Jake dashed to the artifacts as fast as his sore body would take him. He hoisted one of the blue packs onto his back. Amber did the same, and they carried them to the edge of the woods. The director would come, but Jake was determined to protect the artifacts until help arrived. *Come on, Wes. Hurry,* Jake thought.

Then two strange things happened. First, the director again looked at the kids, but this time he smiled and gave them a thumbs up. Amber and Jake looked at each other, both confused by the gesture.

"What was that all about?" Jake asked.

Amber shook her head.

Next, Ranger Trujillo appeared on the ridge and

walked straight up to the director, shook his hand, and began talking.

Amber's eyes narrowed in confusion. "What do you think is going on?"

"I've got no idea." Jake searched his mind, hoping that something might click, but nothing he could find in his memory made sense of what they were witnessing. "Ranger Trujillo is working with the director?"

They watched as Trujillo handcuffed Claymont, then pulled the radio from his belt and talked into the receiver. Securing the radio to his belt, he went back to the director, who was standing relaxed with his hands in his pockets.

Jake nervously gripped the top of the blue bag. "I think we need to be ready to hide the bags and run."

The director pointed up the hillside to the spot where he and Amber stood. Ranger Trujillo nodded, saw the kids, and signaled for them to come down.

"What do we do?" Amber asked.

"I think we have to go," he replied. "But we keep the bags here where they're safe."

Leaving the artifacts at the edge of the woods, they walked down the slope. But when they got to the bottom, they kept their distance. They didn't know who to trust anymore.

Adrenaline still coursed through Jake's body, buzzing like electricity in his veins. If he had to, he would sprint back and hide the artifacts in the woods. From somewhere deep inside, he found the courage to speak.

"Ranger Trujillo, we heard the whole thing." Jake pointed at the director. "That guy is the *director* you heard the two looters talking about yesterday. You need to arrest him, too."

The director took off his sunglasses. His eyes were gray as smoke. It was Gus!

Jake raked a hand through his hair. "What—what's going on?"

"I've been helping Ranger Trujillo with this case," Gus said. "We'll explain it all when we get this guy—and those packs of artifacts—back down to the trailhead."

Still hesitant, Jake and Amber looked at Ranger Trujillo.

"It's okay. He's with us," the ranger explained. "We'll fill you in soon, but you can trust him." He reached to his belt, pulled off a closed knife, and threw it to Jake. "Use that to cut those straps."

He and Amber ran back to the bags and cut them free from the straps.

Amber hoisted one of the bags onto her back. But Jake stood still, looking uphill.

"What is it, Jake?"

"We need to find the spearhead."

"I think I know where he hid it." Amber set the artifacts gently back on the ground. "I'll show you."

As they trudged up the hill, Jake spied Claymont's shovel and picked it up. He followed Amber as she wove a path between the trees deeper into the woods, where the ground was covered in orange pine needles.

"It was somewhere around here," she said. "I had to stay back pretty far so he wouldn't see me, so I can't tell you the exact spot. But we're close."

Something rustled high in the top of one of the nearby trees, then a streak of black fur scurried down the trunk.

"It's one of those squirrels again," Jake said. "This one looks even bigger than the one we saw on the Sand Ramp Trail. Remember, you were going to look it up and find its name."

"I did. His name is Harold." Amber grinned.

Jake shook his head. "Oh my gosh. You're starting to sound like Wes."

"I totally forgot to look it up," she explained. "I promise, I'll find out what they're called when we get back to camp."

They watched as the giant, black squirrel bounded over the forest floor. It stopped under the branches of a tree and began sniffing around, pawing in the layer of duff made up of pine needles, dirt, and leaves.

"Check it out," Jake said. "I think he led us to it. See

how the pine needles and stuff are scattered around." He pointed to a spot of earth. "You can tell someone messed with the ground right there."

They walked closer. Uncomfortable with their presence, the squirrel scuttled up a tree and watched them from its perch. Kicking some of the pine needles away with his foot, Jake stuck the shovel into the dark, black earth.

"Be gentle so that you don't damage it."

"Good idea," Jake replied.

They heard Gus's faint voice calling out from below. "Amber! Jake! Where are you guys?"

"I'll go tell them that you'll be coming soon." Amber sped out of the woods and back down the hill.

Jake kept digging, mounding up a pile of dirt beside the tree. Then he hit something. On inspection, it turned out to be the shallow roots of the pine tree. He had dug as deep as the roots would allow, so he decided to widen the hole. A few minutes later, it was as wide as a car tire—but no spearhead.

He paused, leaned on the shovel, and scanned the forest floor to see if there was another spot where the needles and leaves had been disturbed. But everywhere around him, the ground looked the same.

He continued to dig, widening the hole and piling more and more dirt onto the mound beside it. Then a clump of dirt rolled off his shovel and back into the pit.

Jake picked up the clod. It was heavy. He peeled away the dirt from the surface until a spot revealed a metallic gleam. Cleaning away the rest of the dirt, he worked at uncovering the object until he could see the full surface of the silver spearhead resting in his hands.

Jake stood alone in the woods, holding his breath, his hands shaking. The whole world around him felt like it was vibrating.

He studied the markings carved into the silver surface of the spearhead. Though he couldn't read them, he knew in his gut that the symbols told a story. Half of that story was drawn into the journal secreted away in his camper. The other half lay in his hands.

How easy it would be to slide the spearhead into his back pocket and walk back down the hillside. He could tell them he wasn't able to find it.

But it wasn't his to keep. Lying and taking the spearhead would make him no better than a looter—like Jeff Claymont and the others. It belonged to the park. It belonged not to any *one* person but to everyone.

The black squirrel studied him from a pine bough.

But wasn't this why Grandpa sent us on this scavenger hunt? Wasn't it to find this thing? Jake turned to look behind him, checking to see if anyone was watching, then he slipped the spearhead into his back pocket.

He filled the hole back in, threw the shovel over his

shoulder, and hiked back through the woods. From the top of the hill, he could see a medic team gathered around Jeff Claymont, putting his leg into a splint. Agent Colter had arrived and was talking with Ranger Trujillo and Gus. Wes and Uncle Brian stood beside Amber. Jake could tell by her gestures that she was reenacting the moment he had jumped and rescued the artifacts from the runaway boulder.

As he walked down the hillsides, Jake could feel his heart pumping blood through his body to his feet. His fingers throbbed. The spearhead in his pocket felt like it was growing heavier with each step.

Agent Colter looked at him and smiled. He tried to smile back but couldn't. She returned to her conversation with Ranger Trujillo.

Reaching back, Jake ran a thumb along the opening of his back pocket. He took a deep breath in through his nose and thought. *Grandpa, what would you do?*

"Agent Colter..." he began.

She turned to Jake.

"I...I...wanted to—" before he could find the words or change his mind, Jake plunged his hand into his back pocket, pulled out the spearhead, and handed it to her.

CHAPTER 25

INSTANT REPLAY

An ambulance and two sheriff's vehicles were parked at the trailhead. After the medic cleaned the abrasions on Jake's knees and arms, Ranger Trujillo called everyone over for a meeting. He lowered the tailgate on his truck and invited Jake and Amber to sit beside him. Their parents had gathered several camp chairs into a semi-circle facing the truck. Agent Colter was also there, along with Gus and the two county sheriff deputies.

Trujillo dusted some dirt from his pant legs and cleared his throat. "I'd like to debrief the situation we all just experienced. At noon today, I arrived here with Amber, Wes, and Jake. Around twelve forty-five, the three kids began a hike up to Zapata Falls. A few minutes later, I left and began my drive into Mosca to run an errand before returning to the ranger station."

He looked to Wes, who was standing beside his parents. "Wes, how about you tell us what happened when you three got to the waterfall."

Wes straightened and took a step forward. "When we got to the falls, we noticed a man there. We recognized him right away as the third looter—Jeff Claymont—so we left the waterfall. I decided to run for help. But when I got back to the parking lot, Ranger Trujillo was gone. I told my dad, and we started heading up the trail. That's when Gus pulled up in his truck."

Ranger Trujillo leaned forward, his hands on his knees. "There's something we haven't told you all about Gus. He's a retired agent with the ATF, the Federal Bureau of Alcohol, Tobacco, Firearms, and Explosives. In fact, he was one of the longest-standing agents in that organization's history."

Jake thought back to the way Gus talked with Jeff Claymont. No wonder he had been so convincing; Gus had years of practice and knew how to play the part.

Ranger Trujillo continued, "Two days ago, when he learned of the looting, Gus asked if he could help with the investigation. Gus, why don't you share what happened next."

Gus nodded and picked up the story. "Agent Colter and Ranger Trujillo had filled me in on the results of the interrogation. They also let me study the note the kids had found. Today, around noon, I was walking out toward the dunes when it hit me. Like you, Wes, I'd figured out the time and date of the meeting, but it wasn't until that moment that I realized *Fatal Plazas* was an anagram for *Zapata Falls*."

Wes walked over and gave Gus a fist bump.

Jake snickered to himself, amused by his cousin's excitement.

Gus continued. "I tried to call Ranger Trujillo, but there was no cell service. So, I jumped in my truck and drove here. On the way, I got a patch of cell signal and was able to reach him. We figured that I'd get here first. When I arrived, Wes filled me in, and I ran up to the Falls. Mr. Claymont wasn't there, and neither were the kids, so I got pretty worried. But I noticed tracks in the dirt leading to a side trail and followed them up into the woods."

"When I came out of the woods, I saw Mr. Claymont standing at the top of the hill." Gus lifted his sunglasses and set them on his head. "Back when I was an agent, I did a lot of undercover work. So, I've had some experience pretending to be one of the bad guys. Because I had read the interrogation report, I knew Jeff was communicating with someone called 'the director.' So, I decided to play the part. I figured that would keep

Jeff talking and give Ranger Trujillo enough time to arrive."

"What I didn't expect was that crazy trap Jeff had set up to crush the artifacts." Gus shook his head with his eyebrows furrowed. "While I was keeping Mr. Claymont distracted, a boulder, half the size of a small car, set loose and came racing down the hill toward the artifacts. Then, out of nowhere, Jake here comes tearing across the hillside and yanks them out of harm's way."

Looking at Jake, Gus's face beamed with pride. He turned to Jake's parents. "That boy of yours has got a lot of courage."

Wes walked over to his cousin, gave him a fist bump, and then squeezed himself in between Amber and Jake on the tailgate.

Ranger Trujillo patted Jake on the back and then picked up the account where Gus had left off. "I got there just in time to hear the boulder crash into the rocks below. Mr. Claymont wasn't as fast as Jake and got caught in his own trap." Trujillo shook his head. "He was lucky the boulder only broke his leg."

"Shortly after that, I arrived on the scene." Agent Colter said, tugging at the brim of her ball cap. "I looked up to see Jake coming down the hillside, his legs all red and bruised. He walked over to me and handed me the silver artifact that Mr. Claymont had buried up in the woods."

Jake was beginning to feel uncomfortable. Then he realized why and decided to speak up. "I didn't do that stuff alone." He looked at Amber, who seemed to be studying her shoes that were dangling over the tailgate. She pulled a strand of hair over her ear.

Jake continued, "Amber figured out where Jeff had buried the silver thing. And she pretty much saved me from pulling that boulder loose the first time I tried to get the artifacts."

Wes offered Amber a fist bump. With a shy smile, she reached out and punched his fist.

"And Wes ran all the way back to get help." This time Jake was the one to offer his cousin a fist bump.

Scanning the people surrounding him, Jake said, "It was a team effort."

Then he addressed Agent Colter, "What will you do with the silver spearhead?"

She took off her sunglasses and held them at her side. "First, we'll have it cataloged and examined by our staff geologist. And because the item was stolen, we'll have some paperwork to complete. Pretty boring stuff but important. My hope is that we'll eventually get permission to place it on display at the visitor center museum."

"How about Mr. Claymont?" Wes asked. "What will happen to him?"

"Because Mr. Claymont has committed crimes against

the US Government," Agent Colter explained, "he is now in federal custody. One of my agents will accompany him to the hospital to get his leg mended, and then he will stand trial for his actions."

Everyone grew quiet. A gust of wind blew through the parking lot, whipping grains of sand and dust into the air.

Ranger Trujillo slid off the tailgate and stood up. "Well, if there are no other questions, then I say we pack up and head back to the park."

Wes raised his hand. His hair, which was always wild, had been tousled by the wind, making him look like a red-haired mad scientist. "I've got one more question."

"Sure thing, Wes," Ranger Trujillo replied. "Go ahead."

"Okay, see if you can figure this out," Wes began.

Jake and Amber exchanged a look. More than a little embarrassed, Jake rested his forehead in his hand.

Amber lowered her eyes and shook her head. "It's another riddle, isn't it?"

"It is," Wes answered, his eyes brimmed with joy. He had a captive audience that included all of the parents, two detectives, a ranger, and two sheriff's deputies.

"A man gets charged with looting in a National Park. The judge lets him choose between three different punishments. The first option is that he can be buried up to his neck in the middle of the desert and left to die. The second one is that he can jump off a mountain and fall two-thousand feet to the rocks below. The third is that he is tossed into a cage with a bunch of black bears who haven't eaten in three years." Wes gave the last part with a snarl. Grasping the edge of the tailgate, he leaned forward, his face dead serious, and asked, "What does he choose?"

The group grew quiet as everyone thought about the riddle. A knowing look grew across Agent Colter's face. "I think I've got it," she said.

"Okay," Wes replied. "Tell us the answer."

"The bears."

"Correct!" Wes replied. Though Wes's voice was excited, Jake thought he detected a hint of disappointment. Maybe Agent Colter had figured it out a little too quickly for his cousin.

"You can tell them why, Wes," she said.

All eyes turned to Wes. The wry expression on his freckled face told them he was going to draw this out as long as possible. As the curiosity grew, he looked around as if the answer might be written on the wind.

"Wes." Jake smacked his cousin's leg. "Stop it. Just tell us why."

"Because," Wes said, "bears who haven't eaten for three years are dead."

CHAPTER 26

1880 – At the Cabin

Emma started as the cabin door was thrown open, revealing the stout frame of Mrs. Herard lit by the yellow glow of the lanterns behind her in the cabin.

"I was beside myself worried about you two," Mrs. Herard said. "Ulysses, the next time you tell me that you'll be back before dark, you..." She cut her words short when the two figures emerged from the darkness into the lantern light. Emma knew Mrs. Herard had expected her husband, not a frail young man who could barely walk.

"Oh, goodness sakes, Emma, who is this?"

"This is Abe. Thunder led us to him."

"Thunder?"

"That's the dog's name. The yellow dog. He belongs to Abe."

"Well, get him in here." Mrs. Herard ushered them through the door.

Emma hooked her arm through Abe's to help steady him as they made their way across the wood-planked floor to a chair at the dining table. He sat down, resting his head in his hands. He was thin, his face ashen, and his lips chapped.

The entire trip down the mountain, Abe hadn't spoken except to ask for water. Emma leaned against the cabin wall staring at the boy. She was itching to know more about him. *Where had he come from? How had he ended up on Marble Mountain before he'd been captured and left to die in the cave?*

"Give him this." Mrs. Herard handed Emma a steaming mug full of what smelled like liquid honey. "It'll revive him so he can eat. Also, I'm not feeding this young man a cold supper. I'll have it warmed up and ready by the time he's done sippin' that." Mrs. Herard looked out the darkened window. "I assume Ulysses is bedding down the horses?"

"Yes, ma'am, he is." Emma sat down across from Abe and placed the mug in his hands.

Abe took a sip of what looked like warm milk. He took a second, longer sip and then poured the rest of the silky liquid into his mouth.

"Thank you, Mrs. Herard." He wiped the sticky substance from his lips.

"You're welcome, young man," she replied. "I figured some cream and honey would bring you back to the land of the livin'."

Emma hoped the time was right to ask him at least one of her questions. "Abe, I was wondering...".

Her words were interrupted when the cabin door swung open. Mr. Herard walked in, hung his hat on the wall, and walked over to kiss his wife. Instead of a kiss, he received a whack on the chest with her wooden spoon.

"That's for leaving me here worried sick all evening." She turned back to stirring the soup on the black, cast-iron stove.

Mr. Herard stood beside her, patiently waiting for her anger to subside. When it did, she turned her cheek to accept his kiss. Just for a second, she let her nose touch his. Then she wiped her hands on her apron. "Well, make yourself useful and get me some bowls so I can dish out this soup." She pointed to the cupboards with the spoon. "If we don't feed that boy soon, he's likely to expire."

Abe had closed his eyes. Emma cleared her throat and tried again. "Abe, I've wanted to ask. How did you get up there on Marble Mountain?"

"Hush, child." Mrs. Herard put her finger to her lips.

"Give the boy a chance to get some food in his belly before you go pepperin' him with questions."

Emma let out a sigh and rubbed her pant legs with her hands. She wanted to say, "I've been waiting for *hours*." But she knew Mrs. Herard would only say, "Then you can wait ten more minutes." So, instead, she said aloud, "Yes, Ma'am."

Mr. Herard took four bowls out of a wooden cabinet. One at a time, he held them beside the pot while his wife filled them, then he placed them on the table.

Opening the oven door, Mrs. Herard brought out a metal pan of rolls and put them in the center of the table. They all sat down. Mrs. Herard stretched out her hands to reach her husband and Emma, and they reciprocated. Abe stared at the three of them holding hands. Emma wondered if the boy had never said grace before. Perhaps his mind was just dull for lack of food. She reached out and grabbed hold of his hand.

Mr. Herard cleared his throat. "Dear Lord, thank you for keeping us safe today in our journeys. And for delivering our friend Abraham from both a pit of darkness and the plans of evildoers. We ask you to bless this food for our nourishment and the hands that prepared it. Amen."

They let go of one another's hands and began eating dinner.

Abe quickly finished his bowl. "Thank you, Mrs. Herard. This is the best chicken soup I've ever had."

"It's my pleasure, young man." Mrs. Herard beamed.

I'm sure it's been at least five minutes, Emma thought. She opened her mouth to speak.

"Emma," Mrs. Herard said, "could you get the young man another bowl of soup?"

Emma stood up and took the bowl. Abe gave her a smile. It was the first time she had seen the light in his eyes, and it caught her by surprise. She stood there for a moment too long.

"Child," Mrs. Herard exclaimed, "don't just stand there. Get the boy some more soup."

Emma turned, walked to the stove, and ladled out the steaming broth. She made sure to scrape the bottom of the pot and gather as many chunks of spiced chicken, carrots, and onions as possible.

Surely, now she could ask. Setting the bowl down and taking her seat, she studied Abe as he tackled this second bowl with a little less fervor than the first.

She tried again. "So, where did you come from? And how did you end up in that cave?"

Abe looked around the table like he was judging how much to reveal. "I've been living up north on a ranch with Mr. Abner Sprague. It's a long story, but I came across a stolen item, an old silver spear point. We took it back to its rightful owner. But the carvings on the object fascinated me. So, before returning it, I drew them into my journal." Abe pulled the journal from his back pocket, opened it to the drawing, and lay it on the table.

Silver Spearhead. Found at Turnover Ranch, May 1880

"Ever since I drew those markings, I've been dreaming about them. It probably seems kinda strange, but I feel like they're calling to me." He picked up a roll, tore it in half, and buttered it with his knife. "Then, a few weeks back, I met an old mountain man named Hank March, and he...".

A burst of laughter erupted from Mr. Herard's mouth.

"You know Hank March?" Abe asked.

"Who doesn't?" Mr. Herard replied. "He's sat at this very table more than once."

Abe smiled and then continued. "Well, Mr. March

knew more about the spear point—a legend passed down from the ancient tribes. He went on to tell me that a couple hundred years ago, some Spanish explorers discovered a cave, deep in the blood red mountains."

"The Sangre de Cristos," Mr. Herard said. "The Blood of Christ Mountains."

"Yes, sir," Abe replied. "While the conquistadors explored the cavern, they discovered gold—lots of gold."

Emma gasped. "So you went looking for the gold?"

"No, I was looking for something else." Abe shook his head. "And turns out that I wasn't the only one looking for it." Abe wiped his mouth with a cloth napkin. "Once Thunder and I reached Marble Mountain, I got the sense we were being followed: sounds in the woods, unnatural stuff. From then on, I had a sickening feeling in my stomach.

"Thunder and I found the red Maltese cross marking the cavern entrance, and we found a way to lower ourselves down using that contraption."

Emma leaned forward on the table.

"Emma—" Mrs. Herard gave her a stern look— "Ladies do not place their elbows on the dining table."

Emma pulled her elbows back so that just her forearms rested on the wood surface.

"We found our way to the chamber with the wooden doors, and that's when things went bad. Something knocked my lantern to the ground. I couldn't see a thing; I just heard voices. Before I knew it, I was knocked to the ground, blindfolded, and being dragged across the dusty cavern floor. I heard the creak of iron hinges and then the strike of a match. I could smell paraffin, and I could see the faint glow of lanterns through the scratchy cloth tied around my head. Then they chained me to the wall."

"What happened to Thunder?" Emma asked.

"They made the mistake of laying him beside me. While they got busy doing somethin' else, I was able to feel around and untie him. I told him to go get help, and he bolted out the door. I later heard some of the men saying that Thunder must have found one of the lower cave entrances." Abe looked down at Thunder, who was curled up at Emma's feet.

"The next day—at least I think it was during the day; it might have been night—a finely dressed man came into the room and removed my blindfold. He introduced himself as Mr. Orson Bull. I could tell he was in charge because all the other men seemed afraid of him. He came up to where I was sitting on the floor, put his nose right next to mine, and demanded that I give him my journal."

Emma squinted. "How did he know about your journal?"

Abe shook his head in bewilderment. "That's a mystery I'm still trying to figure out. I managed to slide it out of my back pocket and push it behind one of the crates. I told him it was up with my gear that I'd left on the mountain."

Abe broke another roll and began sopping up the last bit of soup that remained at the bottom. Seeing this, Mrs. Herard took the bowl from him, refilled it from the pot on the stove, and brought it back.

"Mr. Bull sent some of the men back to Music Pass to search for the journal. When it was just the two of us, he glared at me again and said, 'Boy, you've no idea what you got yourself mixed up in.' Then he started asking me questions about the spearhead. Beats me how he knew about it, but he thrust a pencil and a logbook at me and told me to draw it. So, I did." Abe took in a deep breath. "I knew the markings by heart, but I wasn't about to give them to him. So, I just made up some patterns and drew them. He took the logbook from me, grinning his teeth at me in this really strange way. Then he snuffed out the lanterns and left."

"He just left you there to die?" Mr. Herard asked.

Abe nodded.

Mr. Herard stood and began collecting the empty bowls and plates. "Well, young man, Mr. Bull was right about one thing: you've sure got yourself mixed up in something."

"Abe, what was it you were looking for in there?" Emma asked. "The thing behind the stone?"

Abe hesitated, then reached into his pocket, pulled out the object, and pushed it across the table to Emma.

It was a small wooden cube. Holding it in the palm of her hand, she was surprised by how heavy it felt. She tapped it and could tell it was hollow. Then she shook it. There was something inside, but she could find no way to open it.

"This is curious." She traced her finger along one of the sides of the object. "There are lines carved into it." She reached for Abe's journal and pushed it into the light of the lantern that sat on the table. "These markings—they sure look a lot like the ones on the spearhead."

Abe leaned over to take a careful look at the carvings. "You're right," he told her. "They're not an exact match, but they look so similar; they must be connected somehow."

"We'll need to keep you—and your dog—hidden for a while," Mr. Herard said.

Abe gave a sigh of relief. "I'd appreciate that. I'm sure they'll be looking for me."

Mr. Herard patted him on the shoulder. "That fella you told us about? Orson Bull? He's in charge of the Orient Mine. I've had a feeling that he's been up to something. Heard he's recently hired himself a couple of Pinkerton detectives."

"For what purpose?" Mrs. Herard asked, her voice indignant.

Mr. Herard turned grim. "Before today, I was sure it was to keep the miners from forming a union. But now, I'd say it's tied up with whatever business he's hiding in that cave."

"Will you go back home to Mr. Sprague?" Emma asked.

Abe shook his head and stretched. Emma could see for the first time his sinewy and muscular arms. This wasn't the weak specimen she found in the dark.

"No. I need to go south first."

"How far south?"

"To the Grand Canyon."

CHAPTER 27

LEAVING

"It's called an Abert's squirrel," Amber said. She sat across from Jake at a picnic table back at the campground. Holding a book titled *Flora and Fauna of the Rocky Mountains*, she continued reading out loud: "On average, they are fifty percent bigger than a gray squirrel, getting up to thirty-two inches long from nose to tail."

"Wow, that's so weird!" Jake leaned over to see the pictures.

Amber turned the page. "And we might see more because they live all over in the Rocky Mountains. The book says there's a subspecies called the Kaibab squirrel that lives in a part of the Grand Canyon."

Wes perked up. "That's the name of the trail we're hiking, the one that takes us from the rim down to Phantom Ranch." With his laptop open, Wes continued talking without taking his eyes off the screen. "It's called the South Kaibab Trail."

"I don't feel ready to leave the dunes," Jake mused as he turned to look behind him at the swirling sands and the moving specks in the distance, people walking across the brown and yellow landscape. The sun had set, and the birds had finished their evening songs.

"Me either." Amber closed the book and set it on the table.

"Wes, did you find anything?" Jake asked.

"Nothing." Wes's shoulders drooped. "I've looked through all the footage on our RV security cameras, and there's nothing suspicious. But this was pretty cool."

Jake and Amber got up and gathered around the laptop. Wes dragged the play cursor across the security video until several black objects appeared at the top corner of the screen. He pressed play, and a momma bear lumbered into the campsite sniffing around for food, followed by her two cubs.

"Cool," Jake said. "What time did that happen?"

Wes leaned in to read the numbers at the bottom of the screen. "The timecode on the camera app says around eleven a.m. That's when we were visiting Mrs. Holcomb."

Amber looked behind her at the bear boxes where they had stored their food. "Good thing we had all the food packed up."

"Yeah, I bet they were looking for some lunch," Jake replied.

Amber checked her watch. "We're supposed to be leaving in like five minutes."

"How did it get so late?" Wes looked up at the sky. "And so dark?"

"It's a little thing they call sunset," Jake teased.

Wes glared at his cousin, closed the computer, and slid it into a soft case. "I'm excited to see shooting stars and all, but I'm a bit tired of walking in sand."

That gave Wes the idea to bring the sandboards. He went to the RV and, a few moments later, emerged with his backpack on, attempting to hold the three shifting sandboards over his shoulder. One slipped from his hand, swung around, and fell, smacking him on the bony part of his ankle. He winced and hopped up and down. "Dang! That really hurt." The two other sandboards began to slide down his shoulder, and Jake and Amber ran to rescue him from further injury, each taking one of the boards.

The kids walked around the RV and found their parents sitting at a fold-out table playing a game of dominos.

"We're ready!" Jake called out.

"We'll be done in like two minutes." His dad held up two fingers, making the sign of a "V."

It was Mrs. Catalina's turn. She set down her last domino. "And, I'm out!"

The rest of the parents groaned. They gathered up all the dominos into the game's box and then grabbed their water bottles and jackets. It was getting chilly, and goosebumps rose on Jake's skin.

It was their last night, and it felt fitting to return to the place where their adventure had begun, on the shore of the interdunal pond, hidden away in the middle of sand dunes. After hearing the legend of the warrior and the moon ponds, the kids wanted to see the stars reflected on its surface. Jake, Amber, and Wes led the way, and their parents followed.

In the dark of night, the dunes had become a landscape of swirling blue hills, and the snow-white peak of Mt. Herard glowed in the light of a half moon. When they reached High Dune, Amber pointed out the bright gleam of the pond in the distance. It looked like liquid silver in a sea of blue.

The three kids boarded their way down, and the parents hiked in the trails left by their sandboards.

Soon, the three kids stood at the edge of the pond. Amber stooped down and took her shoes off. Jake and Wes followed her cue and did the same. They could see almost every star in the sky mirrored on the surface of the water.

"Mrs. Holcomb was right," Amber said. "I can see why

people thought these places were special. I feel like, if we stepped into the middle, we'd just disappear into another world."

"Are you sure it's okay to go in?" Wes asked.

"Yeah." Amber beckoned the boys to step further in. "Ranger Trujillo said that the artifacts team inspected everything. So it's okay."

They walked out into the center of the pond, where the water came up just past their knees. It was still warm from the heat of the day. As Jake stared up into the sky, he wondered if he had stepped into a space somewhere between heaven and earth, a thin place where the world felt enchanted. He could feel the warmth radiate from the surrounding dunes. Taking in a deep breath, he let his shoulders relax as he soaked in the feeling.

Soon, the silhouettes of their parents became visible at the top of High Dune. Cresting the rim, their dark figures began hiking down its steep slope toward the pond.

"I still can't believe you gave it back," Wes said. "The silver spearhead."

Jake let out a long sigh. "It was the right thing to do."

"I'm proud of you, Jake," Amber said. "And somehow, I think we'll figure this whole thing out, even without it."

Just then, the parents arrived, making their way to the water's edge. Like the kids, they took off their shoes and waded out into the water.

"I've got another riddle," Wes said.

"Give it to us." Uncle Brian put his arm around his son.

"Okay. I actually made this one up: I can be as big as a house or as small as sand. I go out like a candle when I finally land. What am I?"

As everyone pondered the riddle and stared at the sky, a satisfied smile spread over Wes's freckled face.

"Just wait," Wes said, staring up into the night. "The answer is coming."

And Wes was right. A few moments later, a shooting star streaked across the sky.

"A meteor!" Amber exclaimed. "That's the answer!"

Wes grinned and nodded.

They stood in silence and watched as more stars streaked through the night, their bursts of white falling from the sky reflected in the blue surface of the moon pond. Jake soaked in the moment, imagining that the warrior in the legend—perhaps a thousand years ago—had stood in this very spot, watching the sky come alive with light.

They boarded back down the dunes in the moonlight. Halfway across the dunefield, the dads decided to try out the sandboards. After some entertaining wipeouts, they walked back to camp, comparing their wounds and shaking the sand out of their shirts and shorts.

Back at camp, they lit a campfire, and the three families told jokes and stories until everyone was sleepy and ready for bed.

In the morning, after one of Mr. Catalina's amazing breakfasts, they packed up camp and began their drive to the Grand Canyon. It would be a full day's journey, so the kids asked if they could ride together in the RV.

As they pulled out of the campground, Jake watched the rolling dunes go by and wondered when he might return. He'd explored only a small part of the park, and he wanted to hike up into the mountains and maybe camp along the old Medano Pass Road. Perhaps he'd learn how to climb and rappel so that he could explore the underground tunnels of Caverna Del Oro. Just as they were about to exit the park, Uncle Brian steered the RV into the parking lot of the visitor center, pulled into a parking space, and turned off the engine.

He turned around in the driver's seat to face the kids. "Come on, guys. We've got one quick stop before we hit the road."

They hopped out of the RV to see Jake's and Amber's

parents getting out of their vehicles to join them.

Wes turned to Jake. "Something tells me they know something we don't know."

Jake shrugged his shoulders, adjusted his ball cap, and followed Uncle Brian inside.

As they entered the visitor center, the place erupted with applause. The room, filled with interactive exhibits, was also jam-packed with people. Ranger Trujillo was there, along with Agent Colter. Gus and Bonnie Teller clapped as they made eye contact with Jake. Several other rangers were there, dressed in their green uniforms and Stetson hats, all applauding as the three kids walked into the room. Jake's cheeks burned with embarrassment. He hadn't expected they'd be the center of attention.

"Kids, come over here." Ranger Trujillo beckoned them to the middle of the room, where they lined up beside him and Agent Colter.

"Before you leave today, we would like to honor you guys with a gift." Trujillo exchanged a knowing glance with Agent Colter, who went to a table behind them and picked something up.

Trujillo continued, "You three helped us to discover and recover artifacts of important historical and cultural significance."

Agent Colter stepped forward with three white objects in her hands. "And you helped us to find and apprehend the looters who attempted to take those artifacts unlawfully."

"This is a token of our gratitude." Ranger Trujillo shot the kids a proud smile as Agent Colter placed the white objects into their hands.

The objects were the exact shape of the silver spearhead, but they felt almost weightless compared to the heavy silver object Jake had held in his hands the day before.

"Our resident geologist made a plaster mold of the spearhead and poured these plaster replicas," Ranger Trujillo explained. "They are exact copies of the one you recovered, Jake."

Wes and Amber looked at Jake in disbelief. He held the object in his hands, turning it over to see the markings carved into its surface. He shook his head in astonishment, and once again, applause filled the room.

Jake noticed that Agent Colter had another plaster copy of the spearhead in her hand. She approached Gus Teller, shook his hand, and presented to him the same gift. When the clapping died down, Ranger Trujillo spoke again. "Well, you guys have a long drive ahead of you. It's almost five hundred miles to the South Rim of the Grand Canyon. So, we should let you go."

Jake felt like he should say something. He stood up straight and pulled his shoulders back. "Thank you,

Ranger Trujillo. And thanks for making this such a great time for us." He looked at Agent Colter. "We learned a lot, and we'll always remember you guys."

As the crowd dispersed and people began milling about, Ranger Trujillo put his hand on Jake's shoulder. "Jake, I talked with your parents, and they said I could give you one more thing." His hand went to his belt and pulled the pocketknife from it.

"This was given to me many years ago by a dear friend. When he gave it to me, he said that I would one day pass it on. And that I'd know when I'd found the right person to give it to."

He handed the knife to Jake.

Jake took it.

"Go ahead. Open it."

He pulled on the notch in the blade and opened the knife. Inscribed along the top, he read the word: *TRUE*.

"Jake, your actions yesterday showed your heart—that you're *honest*. And that you care about people—the ones who came before you and those who will follow in your footsteps to experience this place."

At that moment, the knife felt as heavy as the silver spearhead. The metal gleamed in the sunlight that poured through the picture windows of the visitor center.

"This knife now belongs to you. Treat it with respect and care. And when you're old and gray-haired like me, pass it on to the right person. You'll know in your gut when you've found them."

Jake marveled at the gift and looked Ranger Trujillo in the eyes. "Thank you, sir."

He looked back down at his hands. One held the plaster casting of the spearhead and the other the knife. Jake thought back to that thing his grandpa would always say, "Sometimes, when you're doing the right thing, it's a magnet for good stuff to happen."

After saying their goodbyes, they loaded back into their vehicles. Jake and Amber sat across from one another at the RV's dining table as Wes sorted through a bunch of card games in the cupboard. He brought a jumbled assortment over and dropped them on the table. Some of the games were still in their worn boxes, and others were just stacks of cards secured by rubber bands.

"Amber, how about you pick?" Wes offered.

She thought for a second and then grabbed a stack of cards. "Let's start with Uno."

Wes put the other games back in the cupboard, grabbed the Uno deck, and began dealing out the cards.

"So, this woman was sitting in her cabin in Colorado," Wes began, "and a couple of hours later, she stepped out at the Grand Canyon. Where was she?"

Jake shook his head. "You're killing us, Wes. This is like *death-by-riddle*."

"Oh, I think I've got it!" Amber said.

"Already? Really?" Jake hadn't even begun to think of a solution.

"Her cabin is on the Four-Corners. You know, it's where the four states come together: Colorado, New Mexico, Utah, and Arizona. Part of her cabin is in Colorado, and part of it is in Arizona."

"That was a really good answer." Wes sounded impressed. "But I didn't say she stepped out of her cabin in *Arizona*."

"Darn. I forgot; she steps out of her cabin at the *Grand Canyon*." Amber scrunched up her lips, thinking.

"Can we have at least *one* clue?" Jake asked.

"Maybe…let me think." Wes tapped his fingers on the table. "I'm trying to come up with a hint that won't give the whole thing away." He scratched his chin. "Okay, I've got it: The woman is also surrounded by instruments."

Jake's mouth dropped open. "Wes, you've got to be kidding me. A cabin full of instruments? Now I'm more confused."

Wes covered his mouth with his hand, trying to hide the delight that taking over his face.

They played a few rounds of the game, with both Wes and Jake picking up more cards than they had discarded. As usual, Amber was winning.

Having given up on any hopes of figuring out the riddle, Jake decided to introduce a surprise of his own. "I've got a clue," he said, and then waited for his friends to respond.

Wes froze. "Wait. What? How can you have a clue? You haven't figured out the riddle yet!"

Jake reached into his pocket, drew out the leather pouch, and placed it on the table.

"What's that?" Wes asked.

"Before we left Mrs. Holcomb's house, she gave it to me. It's our next clue. It's what we came to the sand dunes to find."

Wes dropped his cards onto the table. "You mean that you've had *the clue* your grandpa wanted us to find since *yesterday*? *And* you're just now telling us?" Wes raised his hands in disbelief.

"Things have been kinda crazy since yesterday, so I thought I'd wait." Jake opened the pouch, drew out the object, and slid it toward the middle of the table.

All three of them studied the wooden cube in silence.

Amber picked it up. She tapped it. "It's hollow—but heavy."

She passed it to Wes. He hefted it in his hand to get a sense of its weight. "It's *really* heavy for being so small." He shook it to see if there might be something inside. "Sounds empty." Wes turned it over, studying the carvings on its sides. "Something about this reminds me of the spearhead drawing in the journal that we found in Rocky Mountain National Park."

Amber nodded in silent agreement. "Jake, did you bring the journal?" she asked.

Jake frowned and shook his head. "It's in the camper."

Wes turned the cube over a few times. "If this thing is hollow, then there's got to be some way to open it." He pulled and pressed, but nothing would open the cube. He handed it back to Jake.

Jake worked on the object for a few moments, then gave up. "It's like the box that Jasper gave me at Rocky Mountain National Park; there's no way to open it."

"Can I try?" Amber held out her hand.

Jake gave her the cube, and she tried a different approach, twisting one of the sides. It didn't budge. She turned the cube and tried another side, then another. When she twisted the fifth side, the panel of wood moved. She looked up at the boys with raised eyebrows. Turning it some more, the other sides of the cube clicked and fell open. But it hadn't opened as they had expected, like a box with a lid. Instead, the entire cube, as if on invisible hinges, unfolded and lay flat into the shape of a cross.

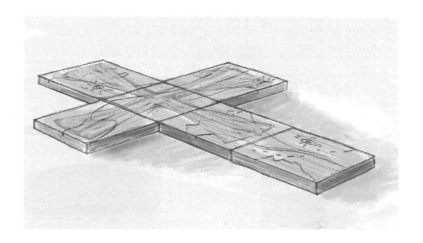

Jake sucked in a quick breath. Wes covered his mouth, and Amber slowly set the cross-shaped object back down on the table. A Maltese cross was painted onto the wood in red and gold. The three kids looked at one another. "So, *this* is it," Wes said slowly, "It's what your grandpa wanted us to find—the thing that was hidden down in Caverna del Oro."

Jake could feel water swelling along the edges of his eyes. Twenty-four hours ago, he had been so afraid he'd miss it, leaving the Great Sand Dunes without the clue his grandpa had left for him to find. He wiped at his eyes before the tears showed.

"So, what do we do with it?" Amber asked.

Wes pointed at his cousin. "Jake, the other day, right before we left Rocky Mountain National Park, your grandpa somehow had that letter delivered to you. It told us what to do next. Did you get anything like that?"

Jake shook his head. "Nothing. But Mrs. Holcomb said that it was some kind of map."

The kids studied the cross-shaped object again.

"I bet the scrapbook will show us," Jake said. He folded the cross back into a cube, twisted the top, and locked it. "We need to look at the Grand Canyon pages. When we stop for a break, I'll get it from the camper."

Wes growled.

"What's wrong?" Amber asked.

"I need something to take my mind off that thing." Wes pointed to the cube. "It's going to drive me crazy." He set his forehead on the table and moaned. Talking into the table, he mumbled, "And the RV has a *full* tank of gas—" he lifted his head— "so we won't be able to stop to get the scrapbook for like *five* hours."

Amber picked up her Uno cards. "How about we keep playing the game? That'll distract you."

Wes sat up and grabbed his cards.

Jake absentmindedly picked up his, too. But he was far away in thought about his Grandpa Evans. Looking back over the last few days, it felt like he had somehow been with Jake the entire time.

"Jake." Wes elbowed his cousin. "Jake, it's your turn."

"Oh...sorry," Jake replied, roused from his wondering. He chose a card and set it on the pile.

Amber gave Wes a playful kick under the table. "How about you give us another hint to your riddle?"

"Okay, I've got *one* more—and that's it," Wes said. "Her cabin...it keeps moving."

"Moving?" Amber's eyebrows furrowed. "Like as in an earthquake?"

Wes didn't answer. Instead, he played his card, leaned back, and waited.

"Okay, Wes," Amber said. "We give up. What's the answer?"

She and Jake leaned forward on their elbows, waiting.

Wes took a moment, obviously enjoying the silence, before giving them what they wanted: "She was flying an airplane."

Chapter 28

1880 - Headed South

Orson Bull sat on his horse at a high point in the foothills south of the dunes. Two men on horseback were beside him, both of them in dark suits with gold badges over the breast pocket of their jackets and bowler hats on their heads. They had holsters secured to their belts and leather rifle scabbards strapped to their saddles. Through a pair of binoculars, Bull studied a figure on horseback. The figure was now miles away in the valley below, trailing a thin cloud of dust.

"Are you sure it's him?" one of the men asked.

"I'm certain."

"Where did he get the horse?"

"Of that, I'm not certain. But the horse is fast. It may be a few days before you catch him."

"We'll apprehend him, sir," the other man said, his voice businesslike and grim.

"Of course you will." Bull handed the binoculars back to one of the men. "That's why I'm paying you. I want the journal and whatever he took from the cavern. And I want you two to keep your mouths shut about this entire business. Do you understand?"

"Yes, sir," both men replied. They whistled to their horses and headed south in pursuit of the rider.

Author's Notes

Visiting Great Sand Dunes National Park

The park is situated in a very remote location in south-central Colorado, and there are not many amenities, even after leaving the park and driving for an hour. If you're camping, there's a great general store a few minutes outside the park that has ice cream, sandboard rentals, groceries, medicines, gasoline, and other items you might need. If you're planning to rent sandboards, go just before the store opens to get in line. Sandboarding can be a lot of fun, but be prepared to have sand in your shoes, shorts, shirt, hair, ears—everywhere. Start on a gentle dune and then work your way up to the more steep and longer ones.

Magnetic Sand? Bring a magnet with you when you hike out onto the dunes. You'll notice (especially after a hard rain) little black specks all over the dunes. This is iron oxide, other known as magnetite. If you run a magnet over the sand, you'll pick up a whole bunch of this fine material.

Piñon Flats campground is a wonderful place to stay. You can reserve sites online at recreation.gov. I really like the views from sites twenty to thirty. If you have a 4WD vehicle, your family can drive up the Medano Pass Road to one of the twenty-one backcountry camping sites. There is no fee to camp here (except, of course, your National Parks entry fee or pass), and they are available on a first-come, first-served basis. You can drive the top of Medano Pass and back down the other side, but you'll need a high-clearance 4WD vehicle. Our family made the trip over the pass in the autumn of 2022, and it was both harrowing and a lot of fun. See our Great Sand Dunes page for pictures and some video: https://nationalparkmysteryseries.com/greatsanddunes

Hikes in Great Sand Dunes National Park

The classic hike in the park is to walk to the top of High Dune (693'). There's no established trail; you just set your eyes on the dune and combine a set of dune ridges to make your route. Avoid the steepest routes to preserve your energy. Depending on your pace, it can take anywhere from two to four hours to make the trip to the top and back down to the Dunes parking lot. Another hiking option that offers some shade is the Mosca Pass Trail. It's about 3.5 miles to the pass, and the round-trip hike takes about four to six hours, depending on your pace. You might also be wondering about the Sand Ramp Trail that Jake, Wes, and Amber hiked. The trail can be accessed from *Point of No Return,* or from loop two of the Piñon Flats campground. Though it's part of the adventure in this story, it wouldn't be my first choice when visiting the dunes. You can find the tree bark peels that Uncle Brian shows the kids at the Indian Grove near Indian Grove Campsite. This is located about four miles up the Medano Pass Road from the Horse Parking Lot. Get more information for planning a trip to Great Sand Dunes at the National Parks site: https://www.nps.gov/grsa/planyourvisit/index.htm

Medano Creek

Medano Creek might be one of the most unusual places you'll visit in your life. The hydraulic force of the creek creates underwater dams of sand that pile up and collapse. This is what generates what's called *surge flow*, small waves that course their way downstream. Though not massive, they are a lot of fun to see (and even better to experience) by getting wet and sandy in the creek. During the snowmelt season, these surges occur about every fifteen seconds.

Because the Medano is dependent upon melting snow

in the mountains, the best times to visit are in late May and early June. However, the place gets packed with crowds, and parking can really be a challenge—especially on the weekends. Camping at Piñon Flats will assure you parking space and enough time to enjoy both Medano Creek and the sand dunes. If you're planning to spend an extended time along the Medano, bring a shade tent to pop up along the sides of the creek. Be aware that the sides of the creek are more sensitive areas where important willow and grasses are trying to take root. Prevent erosion and protect those areas by sticking to the open sandy banks. Fun Fact: *Medano* means "sand dune" in Spanish.

For more information: https://www.nps.gov/grsa/planyourvisit/medano-creek.htm

Zapata Falls

Zapata Falls Recreation Area is about thirty minutes south of Great Sand Dunes National Park. Just as it's described in the story, the waterfall is tucked back inside of a rock-lined ravine. The hike is short to the falls, only 0.4 of a mile. But plan on getting your feet wet because you have to walk through the creek to see it. Like Medano Creek, Zapata Falls is dependent upon snowmelt, and the best time to visit is in the late spring and early summer months. More information at: https://dayhikesnearden ver.com/zapata-falls-hike-colorado/ There's also a great campground on the mountainside near Zapata Falls that provides amazing views of the San Luis Valley and beautiful sunsets.

Caverna Del Oro

I've been up on Marble Mountain, but never to the entrance of what some call *The Spanish Cave,* other known as *Caverna Del Oro.* It's the highest cave in North America, and just one of eleven caves found on this mountainside. Though the cave exists, the legends have never been verified. Back in the 1600s, a group of Spanish explorers allegedly discovered the cave, along with a whole lot of gold inside. The location of the cave became lost, until the early 1900's when a local, Elisha Horn, rediscovered the cave, supposedly finding a skeleton still dressed in Spanish armor, run through with an arrow. There are also tales of locked doors made of oak. The armor, arrow, oak doors, and gold have never been found again—but there is a faint Maltese cross painted in red outside of the cave entrance. Some think the doors are down there somewhere, hidden behind a rockslide, keeping a treasure hidden deep in the belly of the mountain. As mentioned in the story, the cave is dangerous, and perhaps the most dangerous in Colorado, requiring experienced guides who have the proper equipment and knowledge of the caves on Marble Mountain. Watch a video of professional cavers exploring

the *Spanish Cave* at https://nationalparkmysteryseries.
com/greatsanddunes

Ulysses Herard

Ulyssess Herard (1859-1940) was a real settler in the
San Luis Valley. His family had immigrated from France,
and he moved from Kansas to Colorado when he was thirteen years old. He and his family raised horses and cattle in
Medano Park, and even started a fish hatchery where they
raised trout. He was also deaf, having been kicked by a
horse as young man, rupturing both of his eardrums. The
ruins of the Herard homestead can still be found about six
miles up the Medano Pass Road. There are all kinds of
stories told about Mr. Herard: shooting skunk in his
house, getting into a fight with a bear, and all the fun stuff
that comes with homesteading in the mountains. Like
Abner Sprague in book one, he's a guy I wish I could sit
down and get to know.

Prehistoric People and Animals

Imagine a bison (often called a buffalo) that's nearly
eight feet tall, weighing more than 3000 pounds, and with
horns, each three feet long. These creatures roamed the
San Luis Valley until they went extinct about 10,000 years
ago. And they were hunted by prehistoric peoples known
as the Folsom and Clovis. There's some debate as to how
far these cultures go back, but they were living near the

dunes because archeologists have found their spearpoints and other tools at several sites alongside the fossilized remains of *bison antiquus* and mammoths. I like to imagine what life might have been like for these people who likely followed and hunted these through grand landscapes. You can learn more about the Folsom culture, Bison antiquus, and the incredible African-American cowboy, George McJunkins, who first discovered them on Clay Newcomb's Bear Grease podcast: https://www.themeateater.com/listen/bear-grease/ep-28-the-folsom-site-the-amazing-life-of-george-mcjunkin-part-1

Interdunal Ponds

In 1936, more than thirty interdunal ponds were present, mainly on the western edges of the Great Sand Dunes. For dramatic effect, I decided to have Jake, Amber, and Wes discover one in the middle of the dunefield. After 1936, the interdunal ponds began to fade away, and by 1966, they had completely disappeared from the landscape. This is most likely the impact of drought and perhaps over pumping of water from the underground reservoirs called *aquifers*. In 1995, the interdunal ponds made a comeback when several ponds formed again. The hydrology (water science) of the dunes is fascinating. There's actually an aquifer underneath the sand dunes that contains water radiocarbon dated at 30,000 years old! And just like in our story, ancient Paleoindian and Native American artifacts have been found at these ponds. For more information, check out npshistory.com http://npshistory.com/publications/grsa/nrr-2006-011.pdf

The Orient Mine.

At the end of the story, I mention that the bad guy, Orson Bull, runs the Orient mine. I really have no idea who ran the Orient Mine back in 1880, but it is a real place. If you go at dusk, you can sit and watch as a quarter of a million bats fly out of the mine entrance and into the night sky. This requires a reservation with the Orient Land Trust.

Would you let your kids hike alone like the kids do in the book?

To be honest, I wouldn't allow them to hike without adult supervision until they were older teenagers. And I wouldn't ever be comfortable with them hiking solo. There's safety in groups, and most backcountry injuries and deaths occur when people are hiking alone. When we hike as a family, we always stay within eyesight of one another. I think that's a good principle. (Though, I'll admit that it would make for a really boring story).

The Ten Essentials

Day hikers tend to get into more problematic situations than multi-day backpackers. When you think about it, it makes a lot of sense. Backpackers tend to do more planning, and they pack their packs with all kinds of stuff, including food and multiple sets of clothing. I advise that you make a habit of always carrying the Ten Essentials with you, even on short one-hour hikes. You can learn more about the Ten Essentials and purchase the items you need at REI.com.

ACKNOWLEDGMENTS

First, I'd like to thank my daughters, India and Zion, who were the first to hear the story. They gave me feedback and ideas. And they braved the rough 4WD ride over Medano Pass last year. My wife, Jenah, has supported my early morning hours and weekends of writing and illustrating. I'm grateful to my parents, for always encouraging me and helping me to develop my writing and drawing.

Susan Rosenbluth, my editing partner, has helped me to connect with Jake's heart and his heart for his grandfather. Avery Simmons has caught helped me stay true to my voice and what I value as a writer, and to cut what needs to be cut. Kim Sheard provided the first edit, and Anna S. provided the final proofread. I've been blessed to work with such competent professionals.

I'm deeply indebted to all of my beta-readers, especially Lily and Catherine Haws. Their feedback helped me to rework the beacon scene and connect with Jake's emotions. Thank you beta readers: Keziah, Brea, and Matt Toth, Lynn Darah, Ashley Leiterman, Jen Lohr, Hillary

Williams, Michael Murphy, Amy Fritz, Suzanne McNiel, Karen Wittmer, Pattie Smith, and Kelly Moyer.

Author, Jonathan Rogers has been a wise and trusted guide. His writing workshops and retreat helped me sustain the momentum I needed to complete this project. (If you like adventure stories like this one, check out his Wilderking Trilogy).

I want to thank my launch team of educators, librarians, and national park lovers. If you'd like to join one of the launch teams for future books, you can sign up at: https://nationalparkmysteryseries.com/launchteam

Michael Geary's book, *Sea of Sand: A History of Great Sand Dunes National Park and Preserve* was an essential reference. His great storytelling and love for natural history inspired many scenes and gave me all kinds of ideas. In that book, I also learned of former U.S. Congressman, Scott McGinnis, and his tireless work to protect the Great Sand Dunes National Park and Preserve.

Finally, I'd like to thank the rangers who serve at Great Sand Dunes National Park. You protect and help us all better understand the beauty and enduring value of that unmatched landscape.

If you enjoyed the story...

If you enjoyed this story, I would appreciate your help getting copies into the hands of families and other young people. Here are a few ways you can do that:

- **Write a review** on Amazon and Goodreads.
- **Review Writing Tips:** A) Share your experience. What was it like for you to read and experience the story? B) It's a mystery, so try not to post any spoilers. C) If you read the book with a young person, describe what they enjoyed most about the story.
- **Upvote your favorite reviews.** On Amazon, you can *like* the reviews that you find most helpful. This helps to feature those reviews that best serve potential readers.

- **Loan** or give your copy to a friend.
- **Ask your local library** to acquire the series in their collection.
- **Purchase a copy.** They make great gifts. I'll be narrating the audiobooks, so look for those on my author page on audible: https://www.audible.com/author/Aaron-Johnson/B086W2DTMT
- **Post on social media.** You can get links and images to post at https://nationalpark mysteryseries.com/launchteam
- **Share your copy with others.**
- **Connections**: I'd greatly appreciate it if you would connect me with people you know who may be able to help me promote the book and the series. You can make an introduction by emailing me at **aaron@ nationalparkmysteryseries.com**
- By the way, if you promote the books in some way, **email me** to let me know. As a way to say thank you, I've got a small gift to send your way.
- **Bulk Orders:** If you would like to place a bulk order at reduced pricing, reach out to me via email. Bulk orders start at ten books or more.

- **Speaking**: I would enjoy the opportunity to speak via Zoom or in-person with large and small groups. Wilson Rawls, author of *Where the Red Fern Grows*, spoke at thousands of schools. I hope to do the same.
- Visit https://nationalparkmysteryseries.com to discover more ways to engage with the series.

ALSO BY AARON JOHNSON

NATIONAL PARK MYSTERY SERIES

Book 1: *Mystery in Rocky Mountain National Park*

Book 2: *Discovery in Great Sand Dunes National Park*

Book 3: *Adventure in Grand Canyon National Park* - Scheduled for Early 2023 Publication.

Book 4: *Zion National Park* - Scheduled for 2023 Publication.

Book 5: *Yosemite National Park* - Scheduled for 2023 Publication.

Book 6: *Mt. Rainier National Park* - Scheduled for 2023 Publication.

Book 7: *Olympic National Park* - Scheduled for 2023 Publication.

Book 8: *Glacier National Park* - Scheduled for 2024 Publication.

Book 9: *Yellowstone National Park* - Scheduled for 2024 Publication.

Book 10: *Grand Teton National Park* - Scheduled for 2024 Publication.

Into the Rainforest: Book 1 in the Lost City Series

https://NationalParkMysterySeries.com

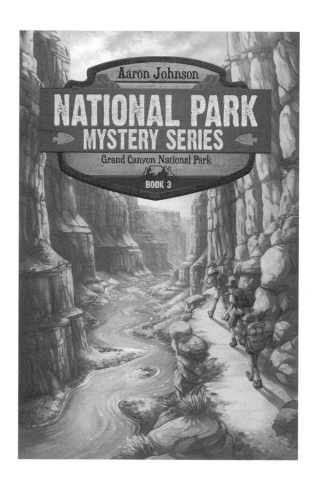

Book Three

Grand Canyon National Park

Scheduled for **Early 2023** release.

Download a draft of the first chapters at

https://nationalparkmysteryseries.com

I'd like to recommend a wonderful book written by my daughter, India Johnson. You can purchase a copy at Amazon at https://amzn.to/3KSj26D or search for Rebels' Daughter.

When twelve-year-old Sky sneaks out one night, her whole

world changes. On accident, she makes an enemy that will stop at nothing to destroy her family and humankind. Her parents are leaders of the rebellion, fighting against those who plan to enslave the last humans. That means that she has to be extra careful. Something she's not. Sky runs from talking wolves and crickcrawks, asking many questions about what's happening to her. Why are her things disappearing? Will she ever convince everyone that she can lead? And when something unexpected happens, she must face the most important question of all. Will she ever get home? Written by twelve-year-old (now fourteen) author, India Johnson, this is her first novel in the *Freedom Through Fire Saga*.

Proud Parent Note: India was the recipient of a Scholastic Art and Writing Regional Gold Key award for *The Rebels' Daughter*.

About the Author

As I've hiked throughout different national parks and my home of Colorado, I've imagined stories about young boys and girls searching for treasure and, in the process, discovering the best treasure of all: the beauty of wild places. I've been inspired by my own searches for a treasure in the gorges and caves of Ohio, and by my dad, who discovered an ancient Native American settlement when he was just a teenager.

I've always loved stories, but I didn't always love reading. That changed in sixth grade when my teacher, Mrs. Jones, gave me a copy of *The Book of Three* by Lloyd Alexander. I hope that the books in my series awaken a love for reading in kids just as that book did for me.

I believe that the best way to care for our natural treasures is to first develop a deep connection with them. I hope you have been able to do so in these pages, and that you'll be able to get outside to develop an even deeper affection for the outdoors and national parks near you.

You can contact me at aaron@ nationalparkmysteryseries.com

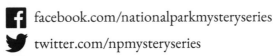

facebook.com/nationalparkmysteryseries

twitter.com/npmysteryseries

instagram.com/nationalparkmysteryseries

Made in the USA
Monee, IL
21 February 2023